Dear Readers

Mistletoe a~~nd~~ ~~holly, carols and cookies~~—and *so* many gifts to shop for! Escape the season's stress with four riveting Bouquet romances guaranteed to restore your goodwill . . . and renew your faith in love.

Scandal and suspense are the name of the game in popular author Jona Jeffrey's Bouquet debut, **Seducing Tony,** when a woman sets out to find the man she believes ruined her father . . . and discovers that passion is much sweeter than revenge. In **Mountain Moonlight,** by talented author Jane Anderson, a single mother's camping trip with her young son becomes a nostalgic journey into her past when their guide turns out to be the one man she could never forget.

But second chances at love aren't always easy. Beloved Silhouette and Loveswept author Suzanne McMinn proves it in **Every Breath You Take,** reuniting a couple whose painful breakup broke both their hearts—but now they must uncover a dangerous criminal before their new chance at happiness is threatened. Finally, first-time Bouquet author Cindy Hillyer sets off **Fireworks** with her tale of two independent single parents asked to plan a kindergarten picnic—only to discover that when they're together the sparks really fly.

So take a few minutes away from the holiday crush to give yourself a gift . . . four captivating love stories from Bouquet.

The Editors

EVERY BREATH YOU TAKE

Miller reached out, each increment of motion his hand made somehow computing to his brain as if it were in slow motion. He couldn't see Natalie's face, could only see her slender shoulders, her thick, straight hair draped down the back of the thick terry robe. The knuckles of her small hand whitened as she grasped the edge of the kitchen counter.

He slid his fingers into that shiny mass of sweet-scented hair, fighting inside himself to keep from burying his face in the back of her neck, from inhaling her feminine fragrance, from tasting the soft skin at her nape, from doing what he knew now that he'd wanted to do when he'd driven over here.

"You're shaking." He nearly lost it when she lifted her head at the sound of his voice, turned, met his eyes. Her gaze was watery, shining with fear, and something else that struck him so hard, he couldn't breathe for long heartbeats.

Need.

More than just need for his protection. Far more than that.

This was need that was basic. Pure woman, pure man. It was the lost, sweet paradise he'd longed for all this time.

EVERY BREATH YOU TAKE

SUZANNE MCMINN

ZEBRA BOOKS
Kensington Publishing Corp.
http://www.zebrabooks.com

ZEBRA BOOKS are published by

Kensington Publishing Corp.
850 Third Avenue
New York, NY 10022

Zebra and the Z logo Reg. U.S. Pat. & TM Off.

First Printing: December, 1999
10 9 8 7 6 5 4 3 2 1

Printed in the United States of America

ONE

Someone had been in her house.

Cabinet doors gaped open. Smashed glass and stoneware littered the tiled kitchen floor. Drawers hung askew, silverware and utensils dumped out. The toaster, ripped from the wall, tilted at an odd angle in the center of the shattered heap, surrounded by a variety of other items swept from the countertops—coffee, cookbooks, fruit, yesterday's mail.

From Natalie Buchanan's position just inside the door leading from the garage of her town house into the kitchen, she stepped toward the living room, her mouth dry, her heart pounding. She stopped in the archway between the two rooms.

Cushions spilled from the couch, artwork and candles and knickknacks scattered over the carpet. The thick, insulated drapes were drawn closed. She knew she'd left them open—because she always left them open during the day. She was a creature of habit, living a life that was routine, comfortable. Safe.

She wasn't safe now.

Adrenaline kicked in, breaking through the ice-cold shock.

Somebody could still be here. Fear rolled over her in a titanic wave.

A soft click-click penetrated her panic. She spun, a half-strangled cry erupting from her mouth. She almost collapsed at the sight of her five-year-old toy poodle.

Prissy. It was just Prissy.

Kneeling to pick up the dog, she squeezed her eyes shut in a second of intense relief. The intruder had to be gone now, or Prissy wouldn't be acting so normal, right? The little dog would be hiding under something if a stranger was in the house.

The relief was short-lived. Somebody *had* been here, between the time she'd left her town house this morning for a meeting with the hospital auxiliary about the upcoming children's wing charity ball and the time she'd returned three hours later.

Could she really be so sure they were gone?

Her gaze shot around, to the hallway, the kitchen, the stairs. Was someone here, somewhere, waiting for her, hiding?

She stepped backward through the kitchen, to the open door to the garage. Then she started running, flying down the three steps into the garage, to her car. She yanked open the door, whisked inside, slammed down the automatic locks, her heart pounding like gunshots.

Prissy whimpered in her arms and she realized she was squeezing the dog's tiny, shaking body too tightly.

Putting Prissy onto the passenger seat, she pushed the remote to open the garage door. The door creaked upward. Prissy yelped as Natalie jerked the car into gear and screeched out of the garage, down the driveway, onto the street. She was out in the open, where at that moment she felt a whole lot safer than in the home that had always been her haven. Parking at the curb, she grabbed the cellular phone out of her purse.

She flipped the phone open and pressed in the emergency 911 number with fingers that felt oddly boneless. She could actually feel her pulse hammering through her veins, the sound roaring in her ears, filling the small car with its frantic beat.

Somebody had ransacked her house. Why?

Did she have something somebody wanted? Or did somebody want *her?*

Nothing made sense. It didn't seem real. Crime was something that happened to *other people*—people on the six o'clock news.

Her gaze darted around the street, paranoia taking hold. Was someone out there, watching her—from a window inside her house, or concealed behind trees or shrubbery? She checked the locks on the car doors again.

She wanted to speak to another human being. Now would be good.

Time stretched, rubbery and meaningless. It

seemed to take hours for the operator to answer the call, though she knew it could only have been seconds in reality.

"Someone's broken into my home." The words tumbled out fast, her voice thin, breathless. "I'm not sure if they took anything or not, but they ransacked my kitchen and living room, and I don't know what else. I was afraid to look around in case they were still there. Can you have a police officer come out here?"

"We'll get an officer out there as soon as we can, ma'am. Please stay calm. What is your location now? Are you still inside the home?"

"No, I'm in my car, parked in front of my town house. I'm calling from my cell phone."

"What is the address of your house, ma'am?"

Natalie gave her the address and the operator repeated it back, then asked for her name.

"Natalie Buchanan. How long will it take for somebody to get here?"

She stroked Prissy as the little dog burrowed into her lap. The bundle of apricot curls felt warm against her own cold body.

"A car is in the area, and the officer is responding to the location now," the operator said. "He should be there in just a few minutes, ma'am."

A few minutes. A few minutes might as well be an eternity.

"Just stay on the line," the operator told her. She continued talking, asking questions, in her calm voice. Natalie supplied the answers while her worried gaze continued to dart.

The street was quiet. Her town house was on a cul-de-sac, and there was generally little traffic, especially during the day. Almost all of her neighbors were professionals in their thirties with no children and careers that kept them away from home during business hours.

A thought slid suddenly, sharply, into her mind. The patio door was unlocked. Was that how the intruder had gotten in and out?

She liked to have her morning coffee outside, on the small, enclosed garden patio. And while she was vigilant about locking up at night, she often went off to work during the day without going back to secure the sliding glass patio door.

She'd always felt so *safe* living in Silver City, Texas, a medium-sized town just south of Fort Worth. It was big enough to boast all the amenities of the city—theaters, restaurants, a state-of-the-art hospital, even a private college—but small enough to lend a certain security that was rare these days.

A certain security that had just vanished, at least for Natalie.

She looked toward the rear of the building. The backyard was full of tall, old trees. Most of her neighbors were at work during the day, and the full burst of spring leaves on the oaks in the yard would have helped shield the intruder from those who weren't.

She caught movement in the periphery of her vision and turned her head. A police cruiser nosed around the corner, moving purposefully toward her. The car stopped in front of hers.

The officer's face was shadowed inside the car, but she knew it was *him.* She wasn't sure if it was the set of his strong shoulders that made her so certain, or the sculpted hardness of his silhouette, or just her own reaction—the way her skin tingled, her throat closed. The awareness was immediate, achingly familiar.

She watched him unfold his strong frame from the car. Even from this distance, the hard blue of his eyes slammed into her. Hard blue that she knew would sharpen into blades of ice when he recognized her.

This was not her lucky day.

But then, she sighed to herself, she'd already pretty much figured that out.

"Ma'am, are you still there?" the operator asked.

' Yes." Her voice was an uneven croak. She struggled to steady it as she picked up Prissy from her lap. "An officer is here. I'm going to hang up now. Thank you for your assistance."

She punched the END button, set the phone on the passenger seat, and got out of her car because she was more scared of the possibility that an intruder might still be lurking somewhere inside her house than she was of the man she'd walked out on ten years ago.

But just barely.

She stood in the street, Prissy squirming in the

crook of her arm, and waited for him to come to her.

"Hello, Miller," she said, desperately grateful when her voice came out normal.

It wasn't as if she hadn't seen him in the past ten years. She'd seen him. Silver City wasn't all *that* big a town.

But it wasn't that small, either. She'd given Miller Brannigan a wide berth. And he'd returned the favor. She'd seen him more than once at the hospital—she'd been there visiting patients in conjunction with her volunteer work. He'd been taking statements from victims.

She'd seen him jogging in the park, checking out at the grocery store, and more times than she could count, she'd seen him in the newspaper— his name, sometimes his photo, in connection with various cases.

They were the same age. He would be twenty-eight. Up close now, she could see his face had matured into stronger, cleaner lines.

He wasn't the part-boy, part-man she'd known. There were light crinkles around his eyes, a slight brush of premature gray at his temples. But that was where the signs of time's march stopped. There was no thinning of his thick brown hair, no extra padding on his hard, lean, six-foot body.

No lessening of the automatic, intense pull his mere presence had always evoked.

His face was a stone mask, revealing nothing. No emotion.

No answering pull of awareness.

"Hello, Nat."

He used her nickname. It tripped off his tongue as if he'd last made love to her yesterday, not ten years ago. It was intimate—but at the same time cold, somehow diminishing.

"You reported a break-in?" he went on.

His tone was flat, professional. He was doing his job. It was as if they hadn't lost their virginity together. They hadn't promised to get married, to love each other forever.

He hadn't told her that he hated her on the day she'd walked away.

They were total strangers.

And that was a total lie, but since this was apparently the approach Miller was sticking with, Natalie went along. Anything else would be a humiliation.

"Well, maybe break-in isn't exactly accurate," she managed. "I think the patio door was unlocked."

"You think?" He stared at her, his blue gaze cool and penetrating.

"I *know* it was unlocked," she said, and this time her voice trembled just a little. "Look, I know that's dumb, so don't bother pointing it out. That's probably how they got in. But what I'm worried about right now is whether they got *out*, okay? Somebody ransacked the place, and after I saw that, I was too scared to hang around—"

"I'll check the house."

Natalie followed him up the sidewalk, onto the narrow front porch. She unlocked the front door.

"Wait here," Miller said. He moved inside, his hand on the gun holstered at his hip.

The sight of the weapon sent fresh fear drumming through Natalie's bloodstream. She held tight to Prissy, who was squirming more than ever.

She stared into the open doorway of the house, waiting endless minutes, her pulse throbbing. What if someone really was still in there?

Miller appeared in the doorway.

"The house is clear," he told her. "I'm going to check the outside. I'll be back in a minute."

Natalie's town house was connected in a block with three others. Miller set off around the side of the building. Natalie went inside and set Prissy on the entry hall floor. The little dog ran around her in circles, barking, her toenails clicking on the marble floor.

"Shh," Natalie tried, bending down to soothe her nervous pet.

Miller appeared in the doorway. "Everything's clear outside."

Prissy yapped at him. He stepped inside the house. The little dog yelped, then ran into the living room and scrambled under the couch.

Natalie straightened. "I got her for a guard dog," she joked nervously.

Miller didn't respond, just took a small notebook and a pen from his pocket. He went straight to business, his gaze level, his tone even.

"There's no sign of forced entry," he said, "so chances are the intruder came in through your patio door, as you suspect. It hasn't rained in several days, though, so there's no evidence of footprints around the rear of the house to bear that out. Did you notice if any valuables were missing?"

"No." She chewed her lip. "I didn't notice anything missing, but I didn't really look, either."

"All right. I'd like to have you do that now," he said.

Natalie nodded. They went through the house together. She wondered if the intruder had looked at—touched—her personal belongings.

She couldn't shake the sickening sensation that someone was watching her, even though she knew that Miller had been through the house already, that no one was there now but the two of them. Looking at the living room and kitchen again, this time she felt a violated anger mixing with the fear.

Nothing seemed to be missing that she could tell. They headed upstairs, where she'd converted two bedrooms into one large one with an attached sitting room that she used as a home office.

"I just can't believe somebody would do this," she started. "I don't understand—"

She gasped, stopped in the doorway of her bedroom, her fingers moving automatically to her lips. Chilling terror swept out the anger.

Her soft down comforter and matching sheets, patterned in burgundy stripes and flowers, had been slashed to ribbons. Bits of stuffing exploded out of her shredded pillows.

* * *

Miller watched Natalie fighting panic, her eyes bright with shock. His heart knotted painfully in reaction—and not for the first time. He'd thought his heart was going to rip right out of his chest when she'd stepped out of her car.

He'd been grateful for the moments it had taken for him to check her house and grounds, alone. He'd used the time to recover, to regain his equilibrium. He didn't want to react to Natalie, didn't want to feel anything for her—except bitterness.

"Is this the first time you've been upstairs?" he asked.

"Yes," she whispered. "I didn't come upstairs before. I was scared, and I just ran back to my car."

"I'm sorry. I would have warned you. I didn't realize."

He watched her struggling to maintain her composure, forcing himself to view her dispassionately. She hadn't changed much.

She still wore her shimmery blond hair long. Her slender, girlish figure had matured, curved, but she still dressed as if she'd stepped out of a fashion magazine. She'd always looked perfect, stylish, feminine, exuding a warmth that was completely opposed to what he knew she was inside. Cold, hollow, heartless.

So why did her frightened green eyes keep tearing at the broken heart he'd spent ten years pretending not to have?

He worked to focus on the scene, on his professional duty.

"Can you tell if anything's missing? Why don't you check that?" He nodded at the jewelry box sitting on her dresser.

Natalie moved automatically and checked it. She didn't have a lot of jewelry because she wore so little of it, and what she did wear was almost all costume. Most of the valuable things she had were given to her as gifts by her father.

The only thing in the box that meant anything to her was a sliver of a diamond set inside a heart hung from a thin gold chain.

Miller had given it to her.

She slid open the bottom drawer of the box. The heart necklace was there.

"Everything seems to be here." She stared at the bed, at the senseless destruction of the scene. "Why would somebody do this?"

She looked at Miller, and saw a softness in his eyes. He wasn't a stranger, at least for this small space in time. She could see a ray of sympathy.

Crazily, she longed to cling to that sympathy, cling to him.

"This looks pretty personal," he said quietly. He indicated the bed. "It seems to me as if someone could be trying to frighten you."

The lump of fear in her throat grew. "Well, if they are, they've succeeded."

"I'm going to need to ask you some more questions," he said.

He was all business again, the softness gone. She had to wonder if she'd imagined it.

Considering the state of her nerves at the moment, no doubt she had.

Downstairs again, they went into the small dining nook, which was untouched, as if the intruder had forgotten it or run out of time. Miller sat down, and Natalie settled in the seat opposite.

"What time did you leave the house this morning?" he asked, notebook propped on the mahogany table, pen poised over it.

"I went to the hospital at eight o'clock."

"You work at the hospital?"

"I'm a member of the hospital auxiliary board. It's a volunteer position."

Miller's eyebrows lifted by a fraction.

Natalie felt a surge of defensiveness. *Spoiled little daddy's girl,* he'd called her once. No doubt he imagined her leading a frilly life divided between superficial patronage to the poor and sick, and shopping and lunching between salon appointments.

She considered not explaining. She'd let him believe she was a spoiled brat ten years ago. If he wanted to think it now, too, then that was probably just as well. Miller didn't need to know about the hours she spent every week visiting sick children, of the love she poured out on them. Of how, in return, they made her feel whole.

There were some things she couldn't explain—especially to him. But pride made her clarify one point.

"I'm employed by Coleman and Brock Consulting," she said. "I work with charities, developing fund-raising strategies."

He jotted the information down on his pad.

"Do you come and go at regular times, keep some sort of schedule someone who knows you would be aware of?" he inquired.

"My schedule varies, depending on the organization I'm consulting for at the moment," she explained. "Of course, the hospital auxiliary board meets on the same day each month. Anyone who knows me would know I'm on the board, and anyone could easily access the dates and times of board meetings. But I can't believe someone I know would do this."

"Somebody obviously did it, and there's a good chance it was somebody you know," Miller pointed out. "Is this the first incident of this kind?"

There's a good chance it was somebody you know. Ice prickled down her spine.

"Yes," she answered.

"No threatening phone calls, letters, arguments?"

"No, nothing." Natalie searched her mind for an explanation for the incident. "I can't think of anything at all."

"Do you have any enemies?"

Enemies? Natalie blinked.

"No."

"What about your father? He could have a few enemies right now."

Natalie stared at him. Justus Buchanan's company, Universal Technologies, was one of Silver City's major employers. Her father had built it from scratch, albeit with old family money, and had resisted takeover bids from big-business adversaries. He'd remained competitive in the ever-changing computer software industry—but not without personal cost to his family.

Natalie had grown up resenting Universal Technologies with every fiber of her being, but she didn't think it was responsible for her latest problem.

"You're talking about the layoffs?" she asked.

The electronics company's recent downsizing had been front-page news. Her father's focus on the bottom line was a subject of local controversy, but Natalie knew in the end that her father would win back the town's critics. Buchanans always did. His father and grandfather had both served repeated terms in the mayoral seat of Silver City, and Justus had an inherent prowess at devoting his goodwill dollars for highest maximum impact on his image.

"I know the cuts are unexpected," she said, "but it doesn't make sense that someone who worked for him would be angry enough to do something like this. He's offering job retraining and extended benefits. Besides, I don't even work out there. I don't have any role at Universal at all, never have."

"You can never tell how someone is going to react to being fired, no matter the circumstances," Miller commented. "If someone was seeking revenge against your father, you could be a target."

He made a notation and went on: "Have you broken up with any boyfriends recently?"

His blue gaze seared her while he waited for her to respond.

"No." She felt herself flush under his scrutiny, the question itself an embarrassment. "I, uh, haven't been seeing anyone. Look, couldn't this just be some bizarre, random act by a stranger?"

"Anything is possible."

Miller flipped shut his notebook and stood. Natalie rose as well.

"I'll take some fingerprints from that patio door," he told her.

He went out to his car and returned with a kit. She watched him dust the door with a fine, charcoal-colored powder. After lifting the prints, he applied the tape to an index card.

"I'm going to knock on some doors, see if your neighbors might have seen anything," he said when he was finished. "If you figure out something's missing, be sure to contact the police. In the meantime, it would be helpful if you stopped by the station, at your convenience, and gave a set of prints. That way, we'll know if the only prints I got off the door are yours."

She walked him to the door, reluctant for him to leave, reluctant to be alone in her town house. But she could hardly beg him to stay . . . and do what?

Hold her hand?

"Thank you," she said.

"Lock your doors from now on." He met her eyes. "I can see you have a security system. Use it."

For just a tiny second, she thought he cared, really cared. And a weak, traitorous part of her heart wanted to believe that he still cared, that no matter how hard she'd tried ten years ago, she hadn't quite made him hate her. Not permanently.

Then she reminded herself that caring about the safety of Silver City's residents was his job. He didn't care about *her*, not on a personal level. She'd made sure that he wouldn't care about her, hadn't she? And it was too late to change it.

She watched him walk away, then shut the door, locking it, leaning against it. Nervous dread prickled through her. She'd worked so hard to be happy, to accept everything that had happened ten years ago, to make something positive out of it.

Now someone had stepped into her tidy, peaceful life. A nameless, faceless someone. She longed desperately to believe the incident was random.

And she was scared to death that it wasn't.

Nobody had seen anything. Miller wasn't surprised. There was an alley behind the town homes. The intruder could have easily entered the neighborhood through the alley, slipped behind the tall fence of the enclosed patio, and come and gone through Natalie's unlocked door.

He got back into his patrol car and drove away. He would check in with Justus Buchanan, see if there were any disgruntled employees acting strangely, if any threats had been made to Universal Technologies that could be connected to the incident at Natalie's.

And then he was going to file his report, and hope he was wrong, that it had been a random incident, that he wasn't going to ever have to get that close to Natalie Buchanan—and her achingly sweet and vulnerable green eyes—again.

She'd looked so frightened. He'd wanted to hold her, comfort her, promise her everything was going to be all right.

But he couldn't do that, even if she hadn't chewed up his heart and spit it back out ten years ago. His instincts were telling him everything was *not* going to be all right for Natalie.

The slashing of her bed reminded him of the overkill of a crime of passion. An out-of-control, desperate passion.

The sort of passion that led to murder.

TWO

Lightning stabbed through the heavy clouds, followed by a resounding thunderclap. Startled, Natalie looked up from her computer and swallowed hard. A second crash of thunder was accompanied by a lashing of rain.

The spring storm shrouded the Coleman and Brock building, located on the corner of First and Fontaine. It was right in the heart of Silver City's restored downtown historic district, with its picturesque architecture replete with the turn-of-the-century flavor that attracted tourists from all over the state. The ornate buildings housed everything from quaint antique shops to cafés to professional offices. The town square had been part of a rejuvenation project spearheaded by Justus Buchanan over twenty years ago, which had resulted in a plaque in his honor within the vaulted corridors of the renovated nineteenth-century limestone county courthouse.

During the same time period, a river skirting the town was dammed to create a lake. Justus had privately lobbied to have the newly created attraction named Buchanan Lake in honor of the Buchanan family's heritage in the area, but it had wound up dubbed Silver Lake for simplicity and political reasons.

Justus had had to settle for the plaque and inclusion in the courthouse tour speech given to local schoolchildren during field trips to the historic building.

Gazing out across the rain-soaked square at the courthouse now, Natalie's nerves danced a jitterbug with each successive boom of thunder. She shut down the program she was working in and turned off her computer. Her office was bright, well-appointed, pleasant—a place she enjoyed spending time in, usually. But against the premature gloom, it seemed suddenly garish, harsh.

Glancing at her watch, she realized that it was past time to go home. She didn't want to walk outside in the rain. She didn't want to go home at all, not after what had happened that morning.

What would she find this time when she opened the door of her town house?

Her phone beeped and she jerked, her pulse skittering erratically.

"Hello, Nat. It's Miller."

Miller's face flashed bluntly into her mind. For a second, just one tiny second, she relaxed, felt safe. Then her chest tightened, squeezed.

Miller was anything but *safe*.

She didn't say anything, couldn't think of anything to say. He went on, his voice professional, devoid of discernible emotion.

"Wanted to let you know that the only prints on the door turned out to be your own," he said.

Natalie had stopped by the police station on her way to work. The officer, a young female with bright eyes and a soothing demeanor, had taken a full set of fingerprints. Natalie had scrubbed her hands afterward, but she could still detect a faint trace of the ink residue on her fingertips.

Being fingerprinted had been a strange experience, not one she'd ever expected to sample.

"Oh."

"I picked up some names at Universal Technologies," Miller continued. "I just wanted to go over them with you, see if you recognize any of them. You got a minute for me to go over them with you now?"

"All right." Her grip on the telephone receiver tensed.

She knew already that he'd been true to his word to ask questions at her father's company. Her father had wasted no time telephoning her afterward, and had spent a solid twenty minutes reproaching her for her negligent attention to security.

Miller read off about ten names.

"These are individuals who reacted particularly strongly to the layoffs, made threatening comments; one of them took a swing at his supervisor. Any of these names mean anything to you?"

She didn't know whether to be relieved or worried. "No."

"I'll interview them individually, check out their

whereabouts during the time the vandalism occurred, but beyond that, there's not much we can do. Even if one of these people can't verify their movements this morning, it's not going to mean much. There's really nothing I can really do but file the report, then wait and see."

A weight expanded in her chest.

"Wait and see?"

"If something else happens."

The heaviness rose into her throat. "Oh."

The steady *rat-a-tat-tat* beating of the rain hitting the roof of the old building filled the next several seconds.

"Be careful," he said.

His voice gentled. Natalie felt a rush of sudden, ridiculous tears, even though she knew the small kindness he showed meant nothing.

She meant nothing, not to him, and she knew that only too well. It was so weak and silly that he still meant something to her.

He went on: "Call the station if anything else happens, or if you think of something."

He said good-bye. Natalie put the phone down, blinked several times rapidly, fighting emotion she couldn't explain even to herself. She reached for her purse just as the door to her office opened a crack.

The office receptionist, Ginny Moore, poked her head in.

"Hey."

"I'm going home," Natalie said.

"I wish you wouldn't. I don't like this."

Natalie met her friend's worried gaze. "I don't like this, either, Ginny, but I can't give up my life because of some lunatic."

Ginny came in and slid into the chair across the desk from Natalie. Her thin, pale face, framed by a sleek auburn bob, set in concerned lines.

"I still think you should go to your father's house tonight," Ginny said. "What would it hurt to spend one night there?"

"So speaks someone who has never spent a night at my father's house."

"I know your dad is a little . . . domineering," Ginny tried.

"Try despotic. And not a *little*, either."

"Okay, despotic. But there are worse things. Like wacko slashers in your house. Think about what this nutcase did to your bed, Nat. That's so creepy. How can you go back there tonight?"

"I have to go back there sometime, Ginny. I'm not going to move in with my father again, not even for one night."

She knew Ginny tried to understand the distance she insisted on keeping between herself and her father, but that she didn't quite get it. Ginny came from a large, close-knit but poor family, in which money could have solved most of their problems.

Natalie's family life had been the opposite. Natalie's mother had died in an automobile crash when Natalie was only three months old, and no amount of old Buchanan money could erase the lack of affection in the home in which she'd grown up, a home where the only tenderness she'd ever known had been from nannies and cooks—not her father. Never her father.

And even the nannies and cooks had been temporary. No employee lasted long in the Buchanan household. Justus was too harsh a taskmaster for that.

Natalie had taken the brunt of Justus's critical control, though—and the last thing she wanted to do was spend the night at his house. She knew from experience that the slightest show of weakness would be an invitation to her father's autocratic interference and censure.

She'd finally figured out that it was the only way he knew how to express his love for her. But oh how she wished he could learn to say the words instead.

"Then come to my apartment," Ginny offered. "Or let me come stay with you tonight."

Her friend's invitation was tempting, but along with being frightened about the day's events, Natalie was angry, too. Hiding out at Ginny's apartment felt like giving in, letting whoever was behind the bizarre trashing of her town house win.

"Ginny, I appreciate it. But it's not necessary. I'm going to be more careful about locking up, and about turning on my security system. I was lax about that, and I won't be now."

"You better not be."

"You know this all might be nothing. Miller agreed this was probably some random incident."

Natalie knew she was stretching Miller's words a little, but Ginny didn't need to know that.

"You haven't said much about Miller," Ginny said quietly.

Natalie's friendship with Ginny postdated her relationship with Miller, but Ginny was one of the rare few who knew the whole story.

"There's nothing to say."

"Do you think this is destiny, Miller showing up at your house like that?"

"No."

It felt more like cruel coincidence than destiny to Natalie. She'd believed in destiny once—she'd believed Miller was her destiny.

She knew better now.

Ginny opened her mouth to speak and Natalie stood abruptly, cutting her friend off before she could start in again.

"Stop it, Ginny," she pleaded. "I know you want everyone to live happily ever after, like you and Ethan." After a romantic whirlwind courtship, Ginny and her fiancé, Ethan Parrish, were planning to be married soon. Ethan was on the maintenance crew at Universal Technologies. "But that's not going to happen for me and Miller."

"I'm sorry," Ginny said immediately. She rose, distress evident in her eyes. "I really didn't mean to upset you. Especially not after everything else that's happened today."

Natalie nodded, grateful for the white flag. "I know. Let's just . . . drop it, okay?"

The storm had quieted to a drizzle by the time

she walked outside. Home was only a five-minute drive from her office.

She turned into her neighborhood, her chest tight with nerves. Everything looked the same— the neat yards, quiet streets, attractive town homes. But it all seemed different now. Menacing.

Every shadow, every bush, made her tense with fear . . . and frustration.

The intruder might not have taken anything tangible from her home, but he'd stolen something valuable just the same. He'd stolen her peace of mind. And it made her furious.

She wasn't going to live in paranoia.

Life was much too precious to be wasted that way. No one knew that better than Natalie.

She parked in the garage and went inside. The fresh fragrance of pine clung to the air. Before she'd gone back to work, she'd called the house-keeping service that Coleman and Brock used for the offices. She hadn't been able to face cleaning up the wreckage herself.

They'd salvaged some unbroken dishes from the heap. Everything else in the house had been cleared out or put back in place. They'd also done a general cleaning that had left the town house sparkling.

The rain had stopped completely now, so she took Prissy for a brisk walk in the cool, moisture-laden evening. The fresh air and exercise returned some measure of her well-being. There was a sense of the world being washed clean, and she felt a slight lift to her spirits in spite of everything.

She could almost convince herself that the incident had been a bad dream.

Still, when she came back in, she carefully checked all the doors and windows, then set her security system. The system sounded an alarm loud enough to wake the dead if triggered. She'd set the system off accidentally a couple of times when she'd first moved in, which was part of the reason she'd let herself grow reluctant about turning it on at all.

She closed all the drapes and blinds. The house was still, silent, shadowed.

Despite all her good intentions, she nearly jumped out of her skin when the phone rang.

Her "Hello" came out breathless.

"Natalie? Are you all right?"

"Brad. I'm fine. The phone just . . . scared me—that's all."

"Is something wrong?"

Brad Harrison had been her best friend since childhood, so it didn't surprise her that he would pick up immediately on her mood. She told him everything that had happened over the course of the day, deliberately leaving out the part about Miller. She just couldn't handle hashing through it again.

"I'm coming over," he said when she was finished.

"Brad—"

"Don't argue with me."

"I'm exhausted," she countered honestly. "What I need right now is to make an early night of it. Thank you for wanting to come over, but I'm fine." As eerie as it was being in her town house by herself, she had an instinctive feeling that Brad would only make her more nervous, fussing over her.

"You shouldn't be there by yourself."

"You sound like my father," she said, and she knew Brad would understand that that was no compliment.

In almost every way imaginable, Brad was *not* like her father. Brad liked her for who she was, never criticized her for who she wasn't. He knew too well how important that was. They'd forged an empathic tie years ago from their common backgrounds, their wealthy, loveless homes dominated by overbearing parents they couldn't possibly please—though Brad had tried a lot harder than she ever had.

Brad's father, the president of Silver City National Bank, had criticized him his whole life, though Brad had capitulated to parental pressure in every way. His great-great-grandfather had founded the town's oldest banking institution, and despite demonstrating incredible promise in high school theater productions, Brad had given up his dreams of pursuing a career in acting. He was a junior officer at Silver City National Bank, and would no doubt one day be its president.

That achievement hadn't come free. Accepting the decisions he'd made to please his father had taken a toll on Brad. He'd buried his pain in a secret rebellion, throwing away the money that meant so much to his father by gambling—until the rebellion had turned into an addiction.

Natalie had been there for him through his recovery, just as Brad had been there for her in the times when she'd needed him.

"Every once in a while, your father is right," Brad commented.

Natalie heard the tension in his voice and realized she'd hurt his feelings. "I'm sorry."

"I'm worried about you, Nat. We take care of each other, you know."

"I know," she said softly. "But I'm fine."

She heard him sigh.

"Promise you'll let me know if you need anything," he compromised.

"I promise."

The silence of the house closed in on her again after she'd told him good-bye. After changing into an oversized T-shirt, she set out a bowl of dog food for Prissy, made a sandwich for herself, and curled up on the couch with the remote control.

She turned on a sitcom, comforted by the company of canned laughter. It grew dark outside her curtained windows.

The phone rang again. She got up to answer it.

She didn't hear anything.

"Hello?" she said, muting the television with the remote. The line was silent.

She hung up. Seconds later, the phone rang again. She let it ring four times before picking up.

"Hello?"

There was another silence; then, just before she was about to hang up again, a whisper came.

"I see you," came the raspy, barely audible voice. "I see every move you make."

Natalie slammed the phone down, backed away, her breath coming in sudden hitches. *Calm down,* she told herself. "Calm down," she repeated out loud then, her voice coming out weak and trembly, not at all reassuring.

She raced to the front window, moved the curtain just enough to peek outside. Could someone really see her? Was someone watching her?

The street was empty.

It could have been a crank call, just some kid. Kids made phone calls like that all the time, for kicks. She paced away from the window, fighting to keep her panic at bay.

She didn't believe it had been a kid.

The car rolled to a stop. He turned off the ignition, stared through the dark at the curtained windows of the town house across the street.

He was a fool.

What other explanation was there for him sitting here, in his car, watching Natalie's house? There was certainly nothing logical about the restless need that had driven him from his apartment across town to make sure she was all right.

Miller pressed the tips of his fingers to his forehead in the darkness, rubbed against the ache building there. Try as he might in the long hours that had passed since he'd seen Natalie, he hadn't been able to shake her from his mind.

He couldn't shake the fear in her vivid green eyes, the powerful instinct in his gut that she was in serious danger. The inescapable compulsion to protect her from whatever threatened her.

He'd managed to block her from his mind for an entire decade, but all it had taken was one look and she was back, seared into his soul as if the time that had passed since their last kiss was no more than an hour. He'd given in to the need to see for himself that she was safe, hoping that once he did, he could put her out of his thoughts. For good.

He'd gone to Universal Technologies that afternoon hoping for the same thing, needing someone to ram home the reminder that he and Natalie weren't meant to be, had never been meant to be. He'd known he could count on Justus Buchanan for that, and the old man hadn't let him down. Buchanan hadn't even deigned to acknowledge that he recognized him, but Miller knew he had.

The disdain of people like Justus Buchanan was nothing new to Miller. Neglected and abandoned by parents he didn't even remember, Miller had bounced from foster home to foster home, staying just long enough for the foster parents to be completely fed up with his defiant behavior before being moved to the next.

He'd landed in Silver City his senior year in high school, and no one was more surprised than he when a princess of the town's elite strata asked him to be her date for a school Sadie Hawkin's dance.

She had been so beautiful. So young and innocent. Or so he'd believed. She hadn't cared that he was all but alone in the world, that he was penniless, rootless, directionless, and that he was what people like her father called trash.

She'd looked at him and seen what he *could* be and, with gentle encouragement and sweet support, for the first time in his life Miller had seen what he could be, too.

And in the space of those few golden months, he'd fallen for Natalie and her guileless eyes— fallen as hard as the proverbial rock.

He had looked into those same eyes today and seen that same pure, guileless innocence. And it had torn him apart inside.

He wanted to hate Natalie Buchanan because she hadn't been innocent, she hadn't been guileless. Everything about her, about their sweet, long-past spring romance, had been a lie.

But he was sitting here anyway, watching her house, making certain she was safe. Driven by something inside he couldn't define or understand.

Something he wasn't sure he even *wanted* to define or understand.

Headlights shining on the still-damp street in his rearview mirror roused him from the past. The vehicle pulled to a stop directly behind Miller. He realized it was a police cruiser.

He rolled down his window as the officer approached his car and flashed his light inside.

"Excuse me—" The officer started, then stopped. "Brannigan. What the hell are you doing here?" He lowered his flashlight.

Miller recognized Alan Gilbert.

"There was a break-in at one of the town houses earlier today and I stopped by to check things out. The town house belongs to an acquaintance of mine, and I was a little worried."

He hoped his explanation made more sense to Gilbert than it did to him.

Gilbert nodded back at Natalie's town house. "Must be the same lady. A nine-one-one call came in from a woman who said she'd had a break-in earlier in the day, and now she thought someone was watching her house."

Miller swore under his breath.

"She doesn't know it's me. I didn't mean to scare her."

"I don't know if your car's what she was calling in about. The report was about threatening phone calls," Gilbert said.

Miller frowned.

"Threatening phone calls?" He glanced sharply at Natalie's town house.

He wasn't sure if it was what he'd wanted all along, or if it was the hand of fate. He only knew what he had to do next.

"Let me handle this," he told Gilbert.

THREE

"What are you doing here?" Natalie stared at Miller, surprised. Beyond him, from the rain-slick street, a uniformed police officer closed the door of his patrol car and drove off down the street. The sound of his tires splashing through a puddle as he rounded the corner filled the muggy night.

Miller wasn't on duty, that much was obvious. He wasn't wearing the dark blue uniform of the Silver City Police Department. She'd hoped part of the intimidation, the vulnerability, she'd felt earlier might have originated from the air of authority, power, his uniform inspired. Now she knew that couldn't be true.

Miller didn't need any uniforms or badges to unnerve her. He was standing on her doorstep now, in jeans so faded they were nearly threadbare, and a plain black T-shirt that delineated each muscle of his chest and shoulders. He looked dark, dangerous, more like a criminal than a man of the law.

He was definitely unnerving, no uniform necessary.

"Tell me about the phone calls," he said.

"It was just one phone call. Or one phone call where they said something. I think they called another time, before that, but they didn't say anything so I just hung up. Then they called back. What are you doing here?" she persisted.

"May I come in?" he asked, still not answering her question.

She moved aside. He stepped into the small tiled foyer, wiping his feet on the mat. She shut the door behind him, then turned, faced him.

He stood there, staring at her. She was wearing a long robe she'd hastily pulled on over her nightshirt. The robe covered her completely, but she felt self-conscious, almost naked, under his gaze. His cool blue eyes penetrated, held her.

She tightened the knot of the robe's belt, then crossed her arms over her chest. Music from the television movie that had just come on drifted in from the living room. She fought the flush heating her face as she struggled not to shrink from his hard gaze.

"I was out, driving around, and I swung by to check out your town house," he explained briefly. His gaze was steady. "I had a feeling—"

"What?"

"A feeling something was going to happen. I can't explain it," he admitted.

She blinked. "You were watching me?"

"I'm sorry if I scared you."

"It was the calls that scared me. I'm embarrassed that I had the police come out, though. I panicked."

"You did the right thing."

"Why were you watching me?"

She felt as if her insides were swimming all of a sudden. She met his gaze, staring into eyes rimmed with dark lashes, eyes that were suddenly not shuttered, not cold. Eyes that were warming her and frightening her at the same time.

The peal of the telephone prevented him from answering her question.

Natalie's gaze swerved to the phone. Her mouth went dry.

"I'm going to get it," Miller said.

He crossed the foyer and picked up the telephone in the kitchen. Natalie followed him. The room was lit only by the glow extending from the bright foyer and the subtle illumination from the lamp coming through the open arch to the living room.

"Hello," he said into the receiver.

She watched him in the half-darkness. His huge, broad shoulders seemed to fill up her small kitchen.

Why was he here?

Why would he check on her, sit outside her house and watch her?

The questions had no answers, just like her other questions—why would someone wreck her house in such a bizarre fashion?

Why would someone terrorize her with threatening phone calls?

She felt as if her whole life was careening out of control, and it was an uncomfortable sensation. She needed control, thrived on it.

He put the phone down and turned, his gaze meeting hers across the short space.

"They hung up." She watched him punch in a series of numbers on the phone. "Did you use the call return feature last time?"

She shook her head.

He put the phone down.

"No one picked up." He went over the number sequence with her that engaged the service. "This automatically dials back the number that just called you," he explained. "It's part of your regular phone service, not anything special you have to order. This will log the number on your phone record, and I'll check with the phone company tomorrow. Of course, it won't help us much if it turns out to be a pay phone number."

"It was him. I know it was him again." Natalie's pulse banged. "It's the same person. The one who wrecked my house."

"It was a man? You're certain of that?"

The raspy androgynous voice echoed in her mind. Male or female?

"I'm not sure," she was forced to admit miserably. "It could have been a man or a woman."

"What did they say?"

"They said they could see me, they could see every move I made."

Repeating the words shimmied a chill straight down her spine.

"Nobody can see you. Your blinds are down."

"That doesn't mean someone's not out there watching my house."

"I was watching your house. No one is out there, Nat. Somebody's trying to scare you."

"And they're doing a fine job."

"I know you're scared. But you've got to keep your wits about you, think straight. You've got to do that if we're going to figure out who's doing this, Nat. And you've got to never hesitate to call the police, never feel too embarrassed to report anything strange. Anything at all. Do you understand?"

Natalie stared at Miller. He'd said *if we're going to figure out who's doing this.*

As if they were a team. As if he was planning to be there for her.

Then she remembered that he must mean *we* in the larger sense: *we* as in the Silver City Police Department. That's what he had to mean.

And that knowledge hurt, ridiculously.

She'd held in so much emotion and stress all day. She was suddenly terrified that she couldn't push it back anymore, that she was going to lose it right here, right now, in front of Miller.

Over nothing.

Over a tiny reminder that she was nothing to him, had been nothing to him for a long, long time. It was stupid, really stupid.

Whirling, she gripped the edge of the counter, fighting the surge of pent-up emotion.

"Nat."

He said her name in a whisper, intense and close. She couldn't turn, didn't have to turn in order to know he was right behind her.

She was so scared he was going to touch her. Scared she was going to cling to him if he did.

She'd spent all day pushing everyone else away, convincing everyone else that she was all right. And the one person on Earth she *should* push away, she knew she wouldn't be able to. Not because she was scared, not because someone had called her, had wrecked her house. But because she'd waited ten years for the moment when Miller would touch her again.

And that knowledge was so sharp, so blindingly shocking, so hidden from herself until this very second, that it nearly sent her to her knees.

Miller reached out, each increment of motion his hand made somehow computing to his brain as if it were in slow motion. He couldn't see her face, could only see her slender shoulders, her thick, straight hair draped down the back of the thick terry robe. The knuckles of her small hand whitened as she grasped the edge of the kitchen counter.

He slid his fingers into that shiny mass of sweet-scented hair, fighting inside himself to keep from burying his face in the back of her neck, from inhaling her feminine fragrance, from tasting the soft skin at her nape, from doing what he knew now that he'd wanted to do when he'd driven over here.

"You're shaking." He nearly lost it when she

lifted her head at the sound of his voice, turned, met his eyes. Her gaze was watery, shining with fear, and something else that struck him so hard, he couldn't breathe for long heartbeats.

Need.

More than just need for his protection. Far more than that.

This was need that was basic. Pure woman, pure man. It was the lost, sweet paradise he'd longed for all this time.

The sweet paradise that his mind might have forgotten—but that his heart, his body, had not.

As quickly as he felt the pleasure, he remembered the pain. This was Natalie, the woman who'd walked out on him, thrown him away like so much garbage.

She wasn't paradise. She had been his very own private piece of hell, and he should have his head examined if he so much as *thought* about pointing himself back down that painful path.

He dropped his hand, eased back a step, putting distance between them. He could use some space. He needed to remember why he was here, his official role as an officer of the law.

"I've got some more questions," he said abruptly. "Let's sit down now. You look like you're about to fall down."

And he didn't want to catch her if she did fall. He didn't want to touch her, not again. Touching her once, briefly, had been enough.

The merest connection had ignited a lightning

flash of bittersweet memories and feelings he couldn't risk, he knew that now.

She followed him into the living room. He could see the ball of apricot fluff under the couch. Bright eyes watched him, but the little dog didn't come out.

Natalie sat down on the couch. He seated himself on the other end, not too close. The house was straightened up from the disorder it had been in earlier in the day. The couch, deep with huge pillows, was upholstered in hunter green plaid, and there were lots of wine-colored candles—on the mantelpiece, on the coffee table—though none were lit. A vase of potpourri yielded a sweet fragrance. The clean contrast of the plush antique white carpet, drapes, and walls gave the room a neat, bright ambience even at this time of night.

The coffee table was an old brass trunk piled with magazines. Natalie picked up the television remote from atop the *TV Guide* and punched a button, cutting off a detergent commercial's cleaning promises in cheerful midjingle.

"Let's go over that phone call again," he said.

Natalie repeated the caller's words.

"Could you hear anything in the background of the call? Anything distinctive or familiar about the voice?" he prompted.

Her brows knit as she thought back. "No. I don't know. I was so horrified by it. I just slammed the phone down."

"You should buy a caller identification box and arrange for service with the phone company—

first thing tomorrow. That will tell you where a call originates before you pick up."

Natalie nodded.

Miller went on. "You should let your answering machine take the calls. If this person wants to threaten you, he or she can do it on tape. And the caller identification box will tell us where they're calling from at the same time. The only problem is, if they're calling from a pay phone or out of the area, the listing might not come up on the box. But if they're that far away, at least you'll know they're not calling from somewhere near your house."

"Can't they block their number from the caller identification?"

Miller nodded.

"We can put a trace on your phone, if we need to," he explained. "But if they don't talk to you long enough, a trace isn't going to work. And if the trace comes from a pay phone, they're liable to be gone before we can get there."

"Sounds like there are plenty of ways for somebody to get around being caught," Natalie said, her green eyes darkened, anxious.

"You'd be surprised how dumb some criminals are—and how arrogant." He hoped the person terrorizing Natalie was stupid or arrogant. And he hoped he sounded more reassuring than he felt. The perpetrator had been smart enough not to leave prints on the patio door. "Nat, are you certain you can't think of anybody who could have an ax to grind with you for any reason?" he asked grimly. "Somebody from your past?"

She looked up at him, and he realized then what he'd said, and what she was thinking. The last thing he wanted to do was bring up the past. Their past.

"No," she said quietly, finally, her voice brittle. "I can't think of anybody from my past who would care enough to want to hurt me."

The house was silent around them.

He cleared his throat, blocked everything but the fact that he was a cop and she was a citizen in danger and he had a job to do.

"I want you to keep thinking, all right? And be cautious. Keep your eyes open, wherever you are. This might be all there is to it. Or this might be just the beginning. Take precautions. Use your common sense. Don't be out alone at night if you can possibly help it—things like that."

She nodded.

"Are you going to be all right here tonight?" He stood, felt helpless.

Leaving her seemed so wrong, but he couldn't stay. At least not inside.

"Yes." She rose, wrapping her arms tightly around herself, protective, closed in. She led the way to the front door.

Miller stopped in the foyer.

"Your father's secretary called me just as I was about to leave the station," he told her. "She added one more name to the list, an employee who had a violent outburst when he got his pink slip, damaged some equipment. Ethan Parrish."

Natalie's eyes widened. "Ethan Parrish?" she repeated, her expression blank, then confused. "I know him. Or I know his fiancé, Ginny Moore. She's the receptionist at Coleman and Brock. They're getting married. They're saving money for a house. Ginny never said anything about him being laid off."

"Really?"

"What are you going to do?"

"Give Ethan Parrish a visit, for a start," he said. "Along with everyone else on the list. We're going to figure this out, Nat."

He wasn't sure who he was trying to make feel better—her, or himself. He knew well how many crimes went unsolved—or were solved too late.

He didn't want to think about what *too late* could mean in this case. He was having a hard enough time keeping a professional distance.

"Thank you for coming by. Thank you for checking on me."

Her eyes were so huge and lost. He struggled to keep from touching her. She needed someone to wrap comforting arms around her, hold her.

Once upon a time, in a different world, he could have been that someone.

"Lock up, turn on your alarm," he said, his voice coming out more terse than he'd intended. "Do you have a pen?"

She took one out of the drawer in the hall table

and handed it to him. He scrawled something on
a business card he pulled out of his wallet.

"This is the phone number to the station," he
said. "I put my home number on the back. I want
you to use it if you think of anything that might
help, or even if you're just afraid."

He didn't question why he was giving her his
home number, why *he* wanted to be the officer
she called if she was in trouble. He knew the answer might not bear up to scrutiny.

He gave her the card and returned her pen,
then walked outside, away from her. He hesitated
on the stoop, listening for the solid *snick* of her
bolt shooting home in the lock.

Inside, Natalie switched on her alarm system,
then walked to the front window, her fingers curling over the card. She saw that Miller was still out
there, sitting in his car.

He hadn't turned on the engine. He was just
sitting there, watching her house, a shadow within
shadows inside his vehicle.

She stepped away from the window, relief
swamping her. He wasn't going to leave her. Not
yet, anyway.

Tears gushed from her eyes, and she let them,
knew she couldn't stop them.

Prissy whined at her feet. She picked up the
dog, hugged her warm body close, and sank onto
the couch, drawing her knees up, crying for everything she'd once wanted, had once held so
close in her reach.

It had been her own fault, no one else's, that she'd let it all go.

Regret stuck in her throat. Had she made the right decision ten years ago?

She'd been scared then, too, just as she was now—only for a completely different reason. Then, the terror had lain inside her own body. She'd been so young and so frightened, and it hadn't been difficult for her father to convince her that sending Miller away with a lie was the most caring thing she could do, that to let him watch her suffer would only cause him to suffer as well.

But she couldn't blame her father for that decision. She had been the one to tell Miller the horrible fabrication with which she had sent him away.

It had been equal parts courage and cowardice. She'd been confused and immature, and a little bit afraid of the powerful feelings they'd shared—and how those feelings would stand up to the test of life-or-death treatments. She had been diagnosed with cancer, and her whole world had changed overnight.

Even she wasn't sure anymore what had been in her head at the time. And it didn't matter now.

She'd survived—but the innocence of what she and Miller had had together was destroyed. *She* had destroyed it.

And wishing she could change everything now was just that—a wish. A wild, crazy, fantastical wish. And she'd found out a long time ago that wishes didn't always come true.

"Here's your mail."

Ginny deposited a stack of assorted envelopes, along with a small box, on the corner of Natalie's desk the next morning.

"Ginny?"

Ginny stopped in the doorway, waited.

"Never mind." Natalie shook her head, and Ginny went out, closing the office door softly behind her. Natalie stared after her.

She wanted to ask about Ethan, but the words stuck in her throat each time she tried.

Ginny had always been excruciatingly up-front about her life. She usually gave Natalie far more details about her love life than Natalie wanted.

Her friend's bliss since meeting Ethan Parrish had been in some ways painful for Natalie, but at the same time she'd been terribly happy for Ginny.

Why was Ginny keeping secrets now?

Natalie reached for the stack of mail and thumbed through it. She was keeping secrets, too, she realized. She hadn't told Ginny about the phone calls, or about Miller stopping by to check on her. She just couldn't handle Ginny's questions. The subject was too painful and too confusing.

She couldn't handle talking about something that even she didn't understand. Why had Miller been there, watching over her? It couldn't be usual police procedure to guard a victim of harassment. The SCPD was chronically underfunded and undermanned.

Miller had been watching her on his own time, not Silver City's.

She set aside the stack of mail and picked up the small box. Taking her scissors out of her middle desk drawer, she wondered how long Miller had stayed. He'd still been there when she'd gone to sleep, but the street had been empty when she woke.

Using the scissors, she neatly slit the wide, clear tape on the sides of the box and lifted the flaps on both sides. She folded back the packing paper.

The creature was recognizable as a mouse, though it had been decapitated. A small white mouse, the kind they sold in pet stores at the mall.

A scrap of paper was attached by a straight pin stabbed into its underbelly. Her pulse throbbed as she read the words.

You're next.

FOUR

"Where did you find the box?" Miller kept his gaze leveled on Ginny Moore.

The young woman looked incredibly fragile, her stylish auburn bob forming a stark contrast to her pale skin. She held her slender hands gripped tightly together in her lap as she sat in one of the two upholstered armchairs in Natalie's office.

Natalie had seated herself in the other chair and drawn it close to her friend rather than sitting behind her desk. The small cardboard box and its gory contents remained open on the desktop—a freakish centerpiece to an otherwise bright office.

The workspace was neat, files stacked tidily in a tray on one corner, an English ivy trailing cheerfully out of its small clay pot and down the side of the desk on the other corner. A monthly calendar hung behind the computer terminal, the grid of days attached below a photograph of riotously blooming purple and yellow wildflowers. Miller stood, pen poised over his notebook, waiting for Ginny to respond.

"It was in the lobby," Ginny told him. "Sitting on the bench just inside the door. I wondered what it was doing there, and I went over to check it out. It was addressed to Natalie, so I brought it in."

Coleman and Brock took up the first two floors of the building. It had a native rock exterior, and was one of the first downtown buildings converted from crumbling ruins to usable business space because of its historic significance as the original county jail. School groups toured it regularly to visit the gallows in the rear courtyard. Miller had noted from the directory on the lobby wall that an investment management firm and a secretarial temp service leased space on the third floor.

"The building was already unlocked when you arrived this morning?" he asked.

Ginny nodded. "Mr. Coleman is always the first one in."

"What time did you arrive?"

"Seven forty-five."

"You didn't think that was strange, a box just sitting in the lobby?" Miller asked.

Ginny chewed her lip.

"No, it wasn't strange. We've had delivery people leave things in the lobby before." She bit her lip again and looked at Natalie.

"It's okay," Natalie said. "You couldn't have known it was anything like this."

She placed a hand on Ginny's arm in a reassuring gesture.

"You didn't give it to Natalie right away,

though," Miller went on. It had been after ten A.M. when Natalie had phoned the station. She'd asked for him, and the dispatcher had notified him on patrol.

"No," Ginny answered. "I put it behind my desk. Mr. Coleman called me into his office right away and dictated about half a dozen letters, so I got busy and didn't really think about it after that. We get our mail pretty early here, and I just brought the box in to Natalie with her other stuff."

Miller noted her comments in the abbreviated self-styled shorthand he used, his mind clicking ahead. He'd have to question Albert Coleman and try to define the time frame in which the box was left in the lobby. He'd have the box itself and the threatening note tested for fingerprints, and he'd begin the task of checking pet shops to see if he could find out where the mouse came from.

But he had a bad feeling that none of it would lead anywhere. That the twisted person playing this vicious game with Natalie was too intelligent not to have covered the fundamentals.

"Do you think you'll be able to catch the person who did this?" Ginny looked troubled.

"We're going to do all we can," he said.

He flipped his notebook shut and looked at Natalie. The violet smudges below eyes dark with residual panic told him that she'd had a bad night, and was having a worse day. She looked scared, and it was starting to take a heavy toll on her.

Had she slept last night? The worry was personal, and he knew it shouldn't be.

Protect and serve—that was his job and that was all he was doing here in Natalie's office, he reminded himself grimly. His job.

He shifted his gaze back to Ginny, back to something far simpler than Natalie and all the forbidden feelings she evoked. Back to his job.

"We'll be running tests on the box and the note," he said. "We'll need you to come down to the station and give us a sample of your fingerprints," he explained to Ginny. "Since we've already got Natalie's prints, we can eliminate the two of you and see what else we have to work with."

"All right." Ginny stood. Natalie rose alongside the receptionist.

"One more thing," Miller said. "Your fiancé is Ethan Parrish, correct?"

From the corner of his eye, he detected the stiffening of Natalie's shoulders.

"Yes," Ginny allowed.

"He was laid off from Universal Technologies."

"Yes." She set to work gnawing at her lip again. He noticed she didn't look at Natalie now but stared down at her feet.

Miller went on: "Are you aware that he was involved in an altercation at the plant after he received his pink slip and had to be removed by security?"

Ginny crossed her arms around her thin waist, finally looked up.

"I knew about that," she said, her voice small. "He was upset about losing his job."

Miller noted the flash of caution in the receptionist's eyes just before she dodged eye contact altogether. Cops made people nervous, even if they didn't have anything to hide. The trick was figuring out when people were nervous, and when they were guilty.

"What about you?" he probed carefully. "Were you upset, too?"

"Of course she was upset," Natalie said, abruptly stepping in. "What are you suggesting?"

"I'm not suggesting anything," Miller said evenly, his eyes on the receptionist.

Ginny blinked rapidly several times, then burst into tears. Natalie drew her into her arms.

"Ginny, honey," she soothed gently, patting her back. "What's wrong?"

She shot a dark glare at Miller while she patted Ginny's back. The receptionist sniffled, struggled to contain her emotion.

"I'm all right," she choked out. "I should have told you, Natalie. It just—it hurts too much. I haven't been able to talk about it. Ethan and I broke off our engagement last week."

"I'm sorry," Natalie soothed softly. "Of course that's hard to talk about. I understand." She met Miller's eyes over Ginny's shoulder, her frown an indictment. "Is there anything else you need to ask Ginny?" she asked tensely.

"Thank you for your cooperation," he dismissed the receptionist. She left quickly, shutting the door behind her.

Natalie looked at him. "Do you treat everyone like a felon?"

"I'm doing my job," he clipped out quietly. "Everyone's a potential suspect at this point."

"Not Ginny." She spoke emphatically.

"You're sure about that?"

Natalie stared at Miller.

"Yes," she said firmly. She reached up, rubbed her temples where a vise seemed to tighten with every tick of the clock.

She was angry—furious—that someone was terrorizing her this way. And scared.

And she was taking it out on Miller, who was the last person on Earth who deserved it. He was doing his job, as he'd said.

And that truth made her feel even worse for reasons too stupid to dwell on.

"I can't live like this," she whispered tightly, turning away from him.

She stared out the window toward the spring day outside, its brightness in contrast to the seeping blackness that seemed to be suddenly swallowing up her life. She was shocked by Ginny's revelation that she and Ethan had split up, but the notion that Ginny could be the person terrorizing her was ridiculous.

Wasn't it?

"I can't start suspecting everyone," she said. "It can't be Ginny. Why would she do something like this to me?"

Why would *anyone* do this to her? The question had been reverberating in her mind since the day before.

She pivoted again, her gaze seeking his despite her better judgment. Entreating some magic answer that she knew he didn't possess.

All he could do was point out the grim facts.

"*Someone* is doing it to you. And we can rule out the possibility that it's random."

There was a lineup of empty longnecks on the coffee table in Ethan Parrish's darkened living room, and a fresh one in his hand as he stood facing Miller in the doorway of his first-floor home. The garden apartments advertised themselves as the "ultimate" in apartment living. From what Miller could see over the laid-off maintenance worker's shoulder, Parrish was going for minimalism rather than the ultimate in anything.

The furnishings were sparse, and the orange shag carpet had seen its best days a long time ago.

"What do you want?" Parrish demanded.

He had a slender build, medium height, and bloodshot eyes. He was dressed in a T-shirt and shorts, and didn't look as if he'd shaved in a few days.

Miller flashed his badge and introduced himself.

"Great. Is this about that stupid equipment? Buchanan's going to press charges?" Parrish swore. "Like the guy can't afford to replace it. He ought to have plenty of money now that he's fired a third of the plant just to pad his profit margin."

"I'm not here to arrest you," Miller informed him smoothly.

Relief flashed in Parrish's eyes, followed by wariness. "Then what are you doing here?"

"I have a few questions, if that's all right. Mind if I come in?"

Parrish didn't move. "Questions about what?"

"Natalie Buchanan, Justus Buchanan's daughter. You know who she is?"

He shrugged. "Yeah. I know who she is. What about it?"

"Someone entered her home and vandalized it. Since then, she's been receiving harassing phone calls. And she had a box containing a threatening note delivered to her office."

He didn't bat an eye.

"The world's full of wackos. So what?" His eyes narrowed. "Are you accusing me of having something to do with it?"

"I'm just asking questions."

"Well, I don't have any answers for you."

He moved to shut Miller out. Miller blocked him by placing his hand firmly on the door, which brought him closer to Parrish.

Miller stared him straight in the eye.

"You want to tell me where you were between the hours of eight and eleven yesterday morning?"

"Since I didn't know I was going to need an alibi, I forgot to take notes."

"You can't remember what you did yesterday morning? What about this morning?"

Parrish rolled his eyes.

"Look, I didn't even get out of bed yesterday morning—or this morning—till after eleven, okay? I've met Natalie Buchanan maybe two times, real briefly—and that's only because my ex-fiancée works with her. Sometimes I heard people talking about her around the office because she's Buchanan's daughter, but I don't know anything about her. I don't even know where Natalie Buchanan lives, so I could hardly go break into her place."

Miller ignored his point. It wasn't hard to find out where someone lived.

He hadn't checked yet, but he expected Natalie was listed in the phone book.

"Then you won't mind stopping at the station later and being fingerprinted."

"Can you make me do that?"

Unfortunately, the fact that Miller was taking a serious dislike to Parrish didn't mean he could run him in and have him fingerprinted.

"Usually, innocent people are eager to rule themselves out."

"I think I'll pass," Parrish said smugly. "I'm a busy person."

Miller showed no reaction while a hum of irritation flowed through his bloodstream.

"Your former fiancée is Ginny Moore?" he prompted, the words coming out clipped, cool.

"Yeah, that's her." Parrish cocked his head.

"You might look closer to home if you're looking for someone who's got it in for Natalie Buchanan."

"What do you mean by that?"

"Ginny."

"Why would Ginny terrorize Natalie?"

Parrish snorted.

"She hates Natalie. She was always talking about Natalie's rich daddy, Natalie's designer clothes, Natalie's upscale town house. How unfair it was that Natalie had everything handed to her on a silver platter while she had to scrape by all her life. I always thought it was weird, like she was obsessed with her or something."

He backed off a step, lurched just slightly, and took a swig of his beer. It occurred to Miller that the longnecks lined up on the coffee table probably weren't from the night before.

Parrish went on, suddenly talkative: "She was furious when I got laid off—with me, with Buchanan. She probably blames Natalie, too. Ginny always has to have someone to blame. It's always someone else's fault if she doesn't get what she wants. She comes off real sweet, but underneath it she's a nutcase. I'm lucky I found out before I married her."

Miller tried to superimpose Parrish's dark portrait of a jealous, angry Ginny Moore over the image of the tearful, mousy woman he'd interviewed in Natalie's office. It didn't fit, but that didn't mean anything.

Somebody was presenting a false picture, and

just because Parrish was a jerk didn't automatically mean he was.

As he sat at his desk at the station hours later, he mentally replayed the interviews with Parrish and the other laid-off employees from his list. He'd been able to contact most of them over the afternoon.

The majority of them volunteered to be fingerprinted, and about half had solid alibis for the way they'd spent their time the previous morning. Several had been at retraining sessions at Universal Technologies, or at job interviews in the Metroplex—the sprawling metropolitan area encompassing Dallas, Fort Worth, and dozens of smaller surrounding cities, of which Silver City was on the far outskirts.

One laid-off employee, an accountant named Peter Dodd, had made a crude remark about Natalie's looks that had set Miller's teeth on edge. He didn't have an alibi and had declined to go down to the station. But like Parrish, the fact that he was a creep didn't make him a criminal. Neither did the fact that he'd noticed Natalie was an attractive woman. What was really wrong with the picture was that Miller had actually let the man's comment bother him.

Miller had phoned the three pet stores in Silver City. Only one of them had sold a white mouse in the past week, but it had been to a nine-year-old kid. It would have been a simple thing for the perpetrator to have purchased the mouse somewhere in the Metroplex.

It would probably take at least twenty-four hours for the lab to get the results from the tests on the cardboard box and the note that had been attached to the mouse, but the phone company had made Natalie's records available to him that afternoon.

The call-return feature he'd engaged at her house the night before had traced back to a pay phone.

A knot tightened in Miller's gut. Who was responsible? Vandalism, harassing phone calls, a gruesome delivery—but not one solid lead.

Someone was playing a bizarre game.

Were they toying with Natalie before moving in for the kill? Could Natalie have been targeted by a stranger, some demented kook who got his jollies from stalking and terrorizing women?

Statistics and his gut told him that it was someone she knew, but he would follow up every possibility, which meant that tomorrow he'd have to commence a thorough cross-check of the files for cases with similar elements.

It was time to go home, but he went out to his car and drove to Coleman and Brock instead. Clouds had moved in on the bright day. The early evening air was thick, heavy, portending another rainstorm. He thought about Natalie going home again to her town house, to another sleepless, frightened night.

Don't make it personal, he warned himself again.

But he knew it was too late. When hadn't it been personal?

When had he ever parked outside a victim's home all night just to make sure they were safe?

He raked a frustrated hand through his hair as he sat at a stoplight. He could get the case reassigned to someone else. But he knew he wouldn't do that. He trusted his fellow officers on the Silver City police force as if they were his brothers, but there wasn't one of them to whom he'd turn over Natalie's case.

He had to know she was safe. That was why he'd given her his phone number, wasn't it?

She hadn't needed him ten years ago but she needed him now.

She'd broken his heart. What was he hoping to prove now, all these years later? That she'd made a mistake? That she needed him, after all?

Or was he the one who needed her?

He banged the wheel and cursed at himself for his stupidity, but when the light turned green he kept on driving to First and Fontaine.

Ginny sat behind her desk in the reception area, clattering away at her keyboard.

"Oh, hello," she said, her voice thready as her hands froze over the keys and she stared up at him.

"Is Natalie still here?" he asked.

The receptionist shook her head.

"She's gone for the day. I doubt she's at home, though, if you're looking for her. It's Thursday. One of her hospital days."

Miller quirked a brow. "Hospital days?"

"She goes by the hospital a couple of days a week. Visits the kids."

"She does this on a regular schedule?"

"Tuesdays and Thursdays. Most of the time. She hardly ever misses a day—not unless she's sick or something."

The information left Miller unsettled. He wanted to resist the notion that the selfish, hollow Natalie who'd walked away from him ten years ago was in truth someone real and caring. That she was really the woman he'd believed her to be when he'd fallen in love with her—and that the cruel, heartless Natalie was the one who was a lie.

He remembered the haunted shadows of her eyes and the secrets they seemed to hold. Had there been secrets between them—not just now, but all those years ago, too?

The question had no answer, and he pushed it aside to hone in on Ginny.

"I had the opportunity to speak to Ethan Parrish this afternoon," he said.

"Oh?" Ginny busied herself, gathering a messy stack of files on her desktop into order, her attention seemingly transfixed on her task.

"He had an interesting outlook on the case," Miller proceeded.

Ginny's hands stilled.

"What did he say?" She lifted her gaze to him, her expression blank. Too blank.

"He seems to think you're obsessed with jealousy toward Natalie. That you're angry, bitter. Possibly even vengeful."

Ginny blinked. "That's absurd," she said, fierce suddenly, her vacant expression cracking. "I consider Natalie one of my closest friends, and I hope she feels the same way about me. He wasn't— you're not—suggesting that I—"

She broke off, clutching the stack of files to her chest as she stood.

"Were you in the office all morning yesterday?" Miller pressed.

"I went out for a while. I had to go to the office supply store and the post office."

"What time was that?"

"About ten. It took about an hour to run the errands, and then I took an early lunch after that, so I didn't come back to the office till noon."

She looked pale and drawn as she gripped the files tighter to her chest, and his cop's instinct told him that she was lying. But about what?

It was still hard for him to imagine that this small, fragile-looking woman could really be responsible for the kind of threatening acts Natalie had experienced.

But he couldn't dismiss the possibility. The incidents hadn't taken any real physical strength— just a lunatic mentality. And lunatics hid behind the most normal of facades at times. Miller had lost count of the criminals he'd helped put behind bars while friends and neighbors reported to the press that they would never have guessed their neighbor or friend was capable of such reprehensible behavior.

"You won't forget to stop by the station for those fingerprint samples?" he reminded her.

Ginny nodded wordlessly. He could feel her staring after him as he left the office.

It wasn't far to the hospital. The steel-and-glass structure loomed over the east side of town, outside the historic district and its restrictive architectural stipulations. As he parked in the lot outside the front lobby area, he thought back to the times over the years when he'd spotted Natalie in the halls of the hospital. The instances had been sporadic. He'd been following up, interviewing victims, and he'd crossed paths with Natalie. He'd assumed the instances were coincidences, that Natalie was visiting friends.

He'd always been careful to give her a wide berth. He thought he knew all he wanted to know about Natalie Buchanan, and that he didn't want to know any more.

He'd been wrong.

FIVE

"How well do you know Ginny?"

The question startled Natalie. She hadn't expected to see Miller tonight, especially not at the hospital. She was doing her best to keep some semblance of sanity in her life, and tonight more than ever she'd needed the good feeling it gave her to see the kids' smiles.

I see you. I see every move you make.

Terror had settled into her stomach like a cold stone. And it shocked her to her core that in spite of that terror, she had walked out of a patient's room a few minutes earlier, almost straight into Miller—and felt a spontaneous burst of light-headed desire that had left her staring open-mouthed at him.

Someone was threatening to kill her. Her mind shouldn't be on anything else. Certainly not on Miller Brannigan.

Still, she felt this . . . uncanny connection. Her head knew it couldn't be possible, that whatever connection they had once shared had been severed long ago. But her heart felt it, anyway—and it hurt, like the phantom pain of an amputee.

"I've known Ginny for five years," she told him, training her mind on the issue at hand.

They had moved to a small alcove off the main corridor to afford a modicum of privacy for their conversation. The dinner trays had already been collected and the pediatric floor was quiet.

"I met her here, at the hospital," Natalie went on. "She'd been in a car accident. She was lucky—she wasn't hurt very badly, just had a broken arm. But she was very upset, and I realized after talking to her that she was at the end of her rope. She's from this tiny speck of a town in south Texas—and her goal in life had been nothing more than to get away from it.

"Somehow or other, a friend of a friend had promised her a job in Silver City and she'd spent every cent she had to get up here. I don't know what happened, but the job had fallen through and she was out of money, desperate to find some way to keep from having to go back home. The receptionist position was open at Coleman and Brock, so I urged Ginny to apply for the job, and then I put in a word with Mr. Coleman about her.

"She's a good person," Natalie went on in a hushed voice, crossing her arms and staring at Miller. "A good friend. Why?" A whisper of renewed fear brushed up her spine. "Has something else happened?"

"I talked to Ethan Parrish today." Miller elaborated on his interview with Ginny's ex-boyfriend.

Natalie was shaking her head before he even stopped talking.

"I don't believe it. Ginny's never acted jealous. Never. He's making it up."

"Why would he do that?"

She threw up her hands.

"I don't know," she cried. "I don't know Ethan very well—I've only met him a few times, briefly. But Ginny always talked about how wonderful he was. She adored him. I have no idea what happened between them, but breakups can be messy, bitter."

Her gaze intersected sharply with his. She swallowed hard, and was glad when Miller didn't pick up the topic where she'd left off.

She didn't want to talk about painful breakups. Not with Miller.

He said: "Ginny was out of the office for two hours yesterday morning. And she was certainly aware of your schedule, when you would be out of the house."

"That doesn't mean she vandalized my house."

"No, none of this means she did anything at all," he agreed. "But it means she has a possible motive, and that she had the opportunity. No one else saw that box in the lobby this morning. Only Ginny. That could be a coincidence. But until we know for sure, you need to be careful."

"You mean paranoid," she said, anger rising again at the way some nameless, faceless someone had taken over her life, at the way all her relationships had suddenly become suspect.

"I don't think it's paranoid to be careful until we find out who it is."

Her knees felt rubbery. Somehow, the gravity with which he took her situation only frightened her more.

She didn't know Miller anymore, didn't know what sort of man he was today compared to the boy she'd loved, but she sensed he would not be the sort to overreact. She'd been too impressed with his calm professionalism not to be certain of at least that.

And he believed she was in danger.

"I'm sorry," she said, rubbing her forehead with fingers that she could see shaking as she drew her hand back down. Her headache was back and it was pounding. "I shouldn't be arguing with you. You're just doing your job. It's just . . . It's so hard for me to even believe this is happening. Sometimes, it doesn't seem real. And then other times—"

She broke off, the image of the mutilated mouse swerving crazily through her mind.

A deep breath helped. She pushed back the awful image and looked at Miller.

There was tenderness in his expression and, strangely, that helped, too. Suddenly, another memory tumbled through her mind, the memory of how it felt to be enfolded in Miller's arms.

Warm, solid, secure. Safe.

What she wouldn't give to be held by him right now. Her body craved his touch, reacted automatically to his nearness.

The thought straightened her, as did the realization that she had been unconsciously leaning toward him. She had to gather strength from within herself.

No one could be strong for her. Least of all Miller Brannigan.

And he certainly couldn't hug her.

That she wanted him to, needed him to, was frightening evidence of her crumbling control.

"I was able to check the phone records from yesterday for that call-return trace, and, unfortunately, your caller was at a pay phone," he told her grimly. "Any more strange calls?"

She shook her head. "I talked to the phone company myself today—about the caller ID service," she said. "It's supposed to be turned on by tomorrow at five P.M. I picked up a caller ID box at the store today during lunch, and I'll hook it up tonight. But it doesn't sound as if that's going to help much."

Miller regarded her for a long moment. "You look like this is really starting to catch up with you. Are you all right?"

The continuing light of worry in his eyes made her heart catch. It was genuine human concern— the sort of concern he might have for any victim, she reminded herself.

She hated the blip of desperation that kept rearing up inside her, the yearning for something more, something long lost.

"I'm fine," she lied. "Just a little stressed."

She tried a nonchalant smile, but it felt stiff as

steel on her face. Her stomach was so tight, it ached. It struck her suddenly that part of the discomfort was hunger—she hadn't felt much like eating lunch after the mouse incident.

"I think I just need something to eat," she decided out loud. "I skipped lunch today, and I haven't had dinner yet."

Food couldn't resolve her fear about the threatening incidents, or the pain squeezing her heart every time she looked at Miller. But maybe the physical strength it would yield could help her deal with the other problems.

"Was there anything else you needed to discuss?" she asked him.

"I have a few more questions. I don't want to keep you standing here, though."

"We could go downstairs to the cafeteria." Natalie flushed hotly. "If you don't mind." She felt like an idiot. She hadn't meant to ask him to go eat with her. She could hardly function through a brief conversation with the man.

How could she possibly sit through an entire meal with him and his dark, dangerous eyes?

It was too late, though. The words were already out of her mouth.

"All right. You're through here?"

She nodded numbly. They walked up the hall, past the nurses' station to the elevator. She pressed the lighted DOWN button.

Neither of them said anything. She hoped the elevator car would be full of noisy people, but when it came, it was empty.

They stepped inside and the elevator whooshed toward the first floor. Natalie fixed her gaze on the indicator light over the door that showed what floor they were passing.

The time until the door opened felt like an excruciating eternity—but couldn't have been more than sixty seconds in reality.

The hospital auxiliary volunteers who manned the information desk were already gone for the day, and the gift shop and snack bar were closed. A few people gathered in one of the seating areas, talking in low tones.

They crossed the atrium lobby with its skylights and verdant greenery, and headed down the wide, well-lit corridor that led to the cafeteria.

"Ginny said you do this two evenings a week, come visit sick kids," Miller said, breaking the silence. He told himself he was bringing it up because of the case. He needed to know her habits, the people who crossed paths with her on a daily basis. Not because he was intrigued by her. "That's commendable," he added.

She shrugged. "It's no big deal."

"It's quite a commitment. I got the impression it was something you've been doing for some time."

"A few years," she said vaguely.

"Why?"

She glanced sideways at him, and though she met his gaze, there was something very closed and hidden about her dark green depths.

Something secretive.

"Hospitals can be scary places," she said, fixing her gaze straight ahead as they walked. "Especially for young people. Illness is scary, too. I just try to take their minds off things for a little while. That's what they need—and I discovered that I had the time to fill that need. That's all."

They arrived at the cafeteria. There was a light scattering of nurses and doctors, mostly clustered at tables along the far wall.

He followed Natalie through the line. She selected a pasta salad. He picked up a cheeseburger and they sat down at a table in front of one of the huge plate-glass windows. It was dark outside, and rain poured down in sheets.

A garden dining area was lit by floodlights, revealing circular cement picnic tables surrounded by sections of thick ivy.

He took a bite of his cheeseburger and thought about what she'd said regarding her volunteer work with sick children, and he wondered what the rest of the story was—because he knew without a doubt that there was more to it. But he knew, too, that whatever the rest of the story was, it didn't have anything to do with the reason he was there tonight.

After all these years, Natalie's secrets weren't his business. Not unless they impacted the case.

Taking his small notebook out of his shirt pocket, he laid it on the table beside his plate and focused on the situation at hand.

"What else do you do with your spare time?"

he asked. "I want to know where you go, what you do, on a regular basis."

"Does this mean everything else you've checked into has been a dead end?"

"I wouldn't go that far," he said. "We don't have the results back on the fingerprint tests on the box, but if we come up with anything that doesn't belong to you or Ginny, we'll compare it to any other samples we get in. Most of the laid-off workers from Universal Technologies that I spoke with today were willing to be fingerprinted. Of course, we may not get any fingerprints off the box at all. And I don't have anything solid on any of the people I talked to today."

"Was Ethan willing to be fingerprinted?" She waited tensely for his answer.

He shook his head. "He wasn't exactly cooperative. Except when it came to talking about Ginny. He had plenty to say about her."

Natalie frowned thoughtfully. "I just don't understand what happened. Ginny seemed happy. I never suspected anything was wrong. What did you get from the others on the list?"

Miller went down the list of names. He came to Peter Dodd. He didn't repeat any of the man's lewd comments, just asked Natalie if she'd remembered anything about him since the day before, when he'd gone over the list of names with her.

"No, I still don't remember him," she said. "I visit my father at the office very rarely, but I could have met him briefly and have just forgotten. Did he say he'd met me? Was there something he said that makes you think he could be responsible for these incidents?"

"Not really. I'm reaching here," Miller admitted. "Which is why I want to go back to your habits, places you frequent on a regular basis. Have you come up with any ideas about who could have an ax to grind with you?"

She sighed. "No." Taking a deep breath, she tried to think. "I really don't go out much. I work, visit the hospital. See a few close friends. Go to the gym, the grocery store, the beauty shop. The usual places."

"What about at work? Have you fired anyone?"

"I don't do the actual hiring and firing." She chewed her lip. "Well, I did catch a secretarial assistant hauling a box of office supplies to her car last year. I asked her to return the things, and she did, but she was fired the next week—because she had an attitude problem and was always late. She gave me the evil eye on her way out of the office, and I had a feeling she thought I'd turned her in. But I hadn't, even though I probably should have. She was a single mom, and I felt sorry for her."

She toyed with the pasta, poking her fork into it without taking a bite. Miller asked her the name of the fired Coleman and Brock employee and wrote it down in his notebook. He ate, and jotted down the different companies and charitable organizations she'd consulted with over the past year.

"Eat," he said when he noticed that she hadn't touched her food.

She looked as delicate as a piece of glass, and the last thing he wanted was to see this pressure break her. He didn't want to be there when it happened, tempted to pick up the pieces.

She took a bite of her meal.

Satisfied, he went on with his questioning.

"You said you hadn't been seeing anyone recently." He knew he was raising a subject that was uncomfortable for them both, but he forged ahead.

As a cop, he had to ask uncomfortable questions sometimes, and he couldn't let his former relationship with Natalie prevent him from doing his job properly.

"What about in the past—the recent past," he clarified. "The last few years?"

He resented like hell the fact that he kept noticing how attractive she was. Every time he looked at her, more memories seemed to resurface, swimming around his consciousness almost like fantasies.

But they weren't fantasies. The smoldering, sweet kisses he remembered had been real.

The heartbreak had been real, too, though. In all fairness, he should have been forever immune to the falsity of her beautiful face.

But life had never been fair in his experience.

"I've had casual dates, nothing serious," she said, and as he watched her, her gaze slid away from his. She stared down at her plate.

He was honest enough with himself to admit that her words pleased him, but they also puzzled him. Natalie was too attractive to be alone. So why was she?

The question was far beyond the scope of his investigation.

"It wouldn't hurt to check it out, anyway," he said, carefully training his thoughts to business. "Sometimes casual can be one-sided."

"Is this really necessary?"

"If you want me to find the person responsible for threatening you, I'm going to have to track down every possibility."

"There just isn't anything to track down here. I'm not exactly a party girl. Lately, if I need a date for some social function, I bring a good friend with me. Brad Harrison."

Brad Harrison. The name rang a bell.

"I remember Brad," he said, memory slowly focusing. "He was a friend of yours in high school." He recalled a tall, lanky guy, sandy hair, a hot sports car that he'd liked to rev up in front of the girls.

Miller had had few friends during his days at Silver City High School, and rich kid Brad Harrison definitely hadn't been among them.

She nodded.

"Right. We're still friends. We go out together occasionally—when he's between girlfriends—but it's nothing romantic."

Natalie took another bite of her pasta salad.

Her inability to offer any insight into the situation frustrated her.

She hated being a victim.

"I don't want to be scared," she said suddenly, anger burning inside her, ruining what little appetite she'd dredged up. She put down her fork as Miller's gaze swerved to hers. "I hate this. I hate it. I'm so furious that someone thinks they can just walk into my life and do this to me."

She blew out a frustrated breath. "I just want to *do* something. What can I do? I can't keep walking around terrified."

He opened his mouth to speak, but she cut him off before he even got started.

"I don't mean caller ID and security systems," she told him. "Those things may help keep me safe at home, but they don't do anything for me the rest of the time. I was all but paralyzed from fear and panic today." Emotion swelled up in her throat. "If I just keep walking around, waiting for someone to attack me, I'll go crazy. I need to *do* something."

Miller nodded. "I understand," he said. "I give a class in conjunction with the police department. It's a crime survival training course. It focuses on mental preparedness for dealing with random violence. You might find it helpful. There are two sessions—you can choose mornings or afternoons. It's held at the community center, the first Saturday of the month. If nothing else, it might help you deal with your fear and anger. I teach it on a volunteer basis, and there's no charge to the community. There's a class size limit, though, so call the station and ask to be put on the list."

The first Saturday of the month was this coming weekend.

"All right." She bit her lip. "Thank you."

She stared at him, thinking she'd been so incredibly right about him all those years before. Despite his brooding bad-boy facade back then, she'd always known Miller was a special person, with a good and generous heart.

That he could still be kind to *her*, of all people, spoke volumes about his character.

"You've been extremely . . . nice," she said.

He was lifting his glass to his lips but stopped in midair, the corner of his mouth quirking.

"And you make that sound so unexpected," he responded dryly.

She watched him as he went ahead and took a drink, then placed the glass back down on the table. Some of the tension balling up her insides relented slightly.

"Well, it is unexpected," she said, pushing her half-eaten meal away and sitting back. "Or it's strange, anyway. After all this time, you're the one coming to my aid . . ."

She let the words drift away, embarrassed, the tension winding back up. She wasn't sure what had gotten into her, what she was looking for.

Forgiveness?

A fleeting emotion passed through his eyes, there and gone too quickly for her to identify it. "I'm a police officer," he said finally, quietly. "It's my job to come to people's aid—my prior history with someone has no bearing on that."

She swallowed. This wasn't where she'd wanted the conversation to go.

"How did you end up a cop?" she asked by way of diversion, though she was truly interested in his life, in what had made him into the man he was today.

Miller smiled, a slight curving upward of one side of his mouth, wry and self-deprecating.

"Well, I suppose I could have just as easily wound up in the pen."

"I don't believe that," she said vehemently.

He shook his head. "It's true. I could have ended up in jail. It was only a stroke of luck that I didn't."

"What do you mean?"

Something shifted in his eyes, and he seemed far from the hospital cafeteria as he spoke.

"It started with graduation night," he said. "I was eighteen and finished with high school. The foster care system was through with me, and so were the foster parents I'd been living with at that time. They gave me a duffel bag with my clothes and told me to find my own place."

Natalie blinked. "You're kidding." She fought a tide of painful remorse.

How she wished she could have been there for him!

She pushed back the regret. She'd done the right thing. She had to believe that, couldn't bear to stop believing it.

It would be too painful.

Miller went on. "I had a job pumping gas, so I had a little money—but no place to stay. I lived in my car for a while, but it broke down, and I couldn't afford the parts to fix it. I was pretty mad at the world, I guess. I remember walking to the Express Mart on Highway Fifty-four. I got a pack of cigarettes and sat down on the curb. This older guy pulled up in a Sixty-nine Charger. A classic. I don't even remember what I was thinking, I just remember watching him get out, walk into the store—leaving the car running. I'd never stolen a car, or anything else, before, but I tried to steal his car, only it stalled out."

"What happened?"

"I got lucky," he said, smiling his crooked half-smile again. "I found out I'd tried to steal a police officer's car. He could have hauled me down to the station, but he got me to talk, and before I knew it, he'd taken me home with him." He shook his head. "It's amazing. All those years I spent in the foster system and I finally found a real family in the parking lot of the Express Mart. John and Emily Farrell took me in and set me on the path I'm on today."

"That's an incredible story," she said softly, thinking the name of John Farrell sounded familiar but not placing it. "I know how much you wanted a family, a real family." She swallowed tightly, the memories even more painful than she'd expected. There was a time when she and Miller had dreamed of marrying and building a family together. Behind his tough exterior, she'd discovered the heart of a boy who wanted to love and be loved. A boy who yearned for nothing more than a family of his very own. "Why haven't you married?"

She hadn't noticed a wedding ring.

He cocked his head, watching her seriously. "I guess I just haven't found the right woman yet."

Natalie's heart beat alarmingly fast. She stumbled for something to say, anything.

"John Farrell," she murmured, searching for the link the name seemed to offer in her mind.

Realization clicked.

"Oh, no. He's the officer—"

"He was killed last year. He and Emily were both shot by a teenager in a yogurt shop, the one out there on the Highway Fifty-four bypass. He and Emily had been to Dallas to see a touring Broadway musical. Emily loved musicals. They stopped for a frozen yogurt on the way home, and walked into a robbery. Knowing John, he was probably trying to talk to the kid, help him."

There was bitterness and pain in Miller's voice, but beneath the grief she heard admiration.

"I remember the newspaper reports. You apprehended the teen the next day."

Miller nodded. "I helped organize the department's Cops and Kids Program after that, in memory of John and Emily. Police officers are matched up with troubled teens for mentoring."

Natalie noted the subject switch, and the sheen of emotion in Miller's eyes.

"That's a wonderful tribute," she said softly,

emotion knotting her throat, too. She was so proud of the man Miller had become. "I always knew you would make something of yourself."

Her uneasiness returned then, as his gaze burned into hers, intense, compelling.

"Right." A dark look of cynicism crossed his face as he watched her.

"It's true." That was one thing she'd never lied to Miller about, and she couldn't bear for him to think she had. "I always believed in you. Always."

"Is that why you accepted a year-long trip to the fashion houses of Europe, courtesy of your father, in return for breaking up with me?" he challenged with a stare that stabbed straight into her heart. "Because you believed in me so much?"

He spoke the awful truth—or at least the truth as he knew it. The knife in her heart twisted a little more with every word.

"You don't understand," she said.

He studied her thoughtfully.

"No, you're right. I don't understand." His voice vibrated with tension.

She didn't know what to say. She felt sick.

"We were kids," she said, knowing even as she spoke that the excuse was unworthy of both of them.

Suddenly, she wished for nothing more than to confess her foolish, long-ago deception, but what would be the point?

She wasn't the eighteen-year-old girl who had

loved him so passionately. And he wasn't the boy who had loved her in return.

There was no going back, no matter how painfully and secretly she might wish it.

A long beat passed before he answered. "Yeah," he said quietly, flatly. "We were kids."

He pushed his plate away, stared at the windows, at the black night.

Looking around, Natalie realized that the hospital cafeteria had emptied while they'd been talking. She cleared her throat.

"I've, uh, taken up far too much of your personal time. It's getting late." She reached for her purse, eager to get out of there.

Picking up his notebook, Miller walked with her out of the cafeteria, back up the hall to the hospital lobby. Outside, the rain had stopped, but the air remained damp and chilly.

The parking lot was half-full and still. They stood under the protection of the covered entrance.

"I'll see you to your car," he said stiffly.

"Oh, please don't do that," she said. "I'll be fine. Really." She pasted on a polite smile. "Thanks again, Miller."

"All right. Be careful when you get home."

She thought she saw regret cross his face; then his expression hardened, detached.

"Lock up. I know." Her smile turned rueful.

She stepped out into the night, arms crossed for warmth as she hurried across the quiet park-

ing lot. Cold, moist air stung her cheeks, blending
with the tears she tried to blink away but couldn't.

Looking back once, she saw Miller standing by
the entrance, watching her. She gave him a slight
wave, then turned back. Her BMW was parked in
the second row back, and as she stepped into the
middle of the lane between the rows, she heard
something and glanced to her right.

A car, its headlights off, hurtled straight for her.

SIX

Miller heard the squeal of tires before he saw the dark car. His gaze darted automatically back to Natalie. She was frozen, then lunging out of the way as the vehicle accelerated threateningly toward her. He saw her stumble and go down.

"Natalie!" Then he was running, his cop's mind swinging into automatic.

The car was medium-sized, dark, a basic sedan, probably domestic, but even in the well-lit parking lot, without headlights and from this distance, he didn't have a prayer of making out the license plate.

For a split second, he was tempted to race to his own car, take off after the perpetrator. But he knew that he'd probably never catch up to the speeding vehicle at this point.

And trying to would mean leaving Natalie.

The car screeched wildly around the corner of the hospital complex and disappeared just as he reached Natalie's side. She struggled to her feet, and he reached out to help her. The hand she laid in his was trembling uncontrollably.

"Natalie? Are you okay?" He didn't let go of her, half-afraid she'd fall.

A fierce protectiveness rose inside him. He took in the angry scratches on her knees and hands where she'd hit the pavement. He fought inside himself to maintain his professional objectivity, to keep from pulling her gently into his arms and thanking God that she wasn't hurt any worse.

She stared at him, her beautiful eyes huge and glassy with shock.

"That car," she breathed hoarsely. "It was going to hit me. They wanted to hit me!"

"You're hurt."

"I tripped."

She looked down at herself, seeming to realize only then that she was hurt at all. The soft material of her dress stuck damply to her body where she'd hit the wet pavement.

She lifted her gaze back to his face.

"Wait. They *could* have hit me if they'd really wanted to," she said in confusion. "So why didn't they? Are they trying to scare me—again? Why is someone doing this to me?"

"I don't know, honey. I don't know. Come on. Let's get you inside the hospital. You need to let a doctor check you over—"

"No, I'm all right. I don't need a doctor." She moved her hand from her lips to swipe at the tears streaking her face. "I need—" Emotion broke her voice, the anger draining from her eyes to be replaced by vulnerability. "I need—"

Miller's heart turned over.

Reaching out without thinking, functioning on emotion alone, he touched her shoulder. There was no more fighting it, no more caring what happened next.

He pulled her toward him and she came.

To hell with objectivity.

He wasn't objective, could never be objective with Natalie Buchanan. Who was he kidding? His job had nothing to do with what he was doing now.

She needed him, even if she couldn't quite say it. And he needed her, desperately, fiercely.

Insanely. In spite of everything.

She clutched his shoulders, sharp sobs wracking her slender body. It was both yesterday and a thousand lifetimes since he'd held her this way. She was soft, rounded in all the right places.

The fit of her curves, even her scent—like rain and spring gardens—was familiar, heady and torturous all at once. He cradled her against him, breathing soothing words into her ear.

Soothing who? Her? Himself?

He didn't know.

Blending with his own anguished feelings came rage, dark and unnervingly deep, at the creep who'd tried to run her down. And at himself for not walking her to the car over her protests.

"I'm going to find out who's doing this," he told her grimly, as afraid to let go of her as he was to keep holding her.

In his arms, she was safe.

He couldn't bear for her to be hurt. He

shouldn't care—she was hard and cold and self-ish. She'd walked out on him, trampled his heart.

None of that mattered now. Holding her, he could remember the good times—the innocence with which she'd made love to him, the enthusiasm with which she'd listened to his dreams, and the sweetness with which she'd encouraged him to make them come true.

The rest of it, the dark ending to their romance, didn't even seem real. Yet he knew it was, because he felt his heart cracking into a thousand pieces from the pain of it.

She pulled out of his arms then and stared up at him. "You can't really promise me that you'll catch whoever's doing this, can you?"

He closed his eyes briefly, opened them to face the raw fear in hers. He couldn't lie to her.

"No, I can't promise you that." He drew a deep breath and expelled it. "But I promise you that I'm going to do everything in my power to stop them, whoever they are, from doing anything else."

With one hand, he brushed back the hair waving over her cheek, tucking it behind her ear. He still wanted to touch her, *needed* to touch her.

Lightning forked the sky and thunder rumbled along behind it. The rain started up again.

"Come on," he said briskly, desperately seeking perspective as he forced himself to drop his hand from her soft hair. "We're going to get soaked out here. And I need to report this as soon as possible."

"I want to go home."

He could see her pulling herself together, pushing back the panic. She stepped back, her expression apologetic, embarrassed.

She was still shaking.

"Then you're coming with me," he said, taking charge. "You're in no condition to drive."

She didn't argue, went with him docilely when he took her arm, guided her to his police cruiser.

He opened the door for her and she slid in. He got in on the other side. The rain picked up, pattering on the roof.

She shivered and he reached over, briefly touched her hand. It was icy. He had to force himself to let go of her and reach for the hand-held radio in his cruiser.

He called the station and reported the incident.

Driving out of the hospital parking lot, he checked on her from the corner of his eye. She sat there, stunned, her gaze fixed out the passenger window, her hands in her lap. He ached with the reckless need to hold her again, to comfort her.

"I didn't get the license plate," he said, gripping the steering wheel too tightly in his effort to keep his hands to himself. "Did you catch anything? The make of the car, even a few numbers off the plate?"

She shook her head, turned and met his eyes then. "I didn't notice anything. The headlights were off. The car was dark. Black, I guess." She shrugged disconsolately. "Average-sized."

"Do you know anybody who has a car like that?"

A few seconds ticked by. The windshield wiper blades and the pouring rain kept up a steady swish and staccato rhythm.

"Ginny does," she said tightly. "But it's an older model, and this car didn't look old. It didn't look like Ginny's car."

"I thought you didn't get a good look at it."

"I didn't. But it's not Ginny's." She stared out the passenger window again. "Lots of people must have cars like that. It could be anybody. It could even be a rental car, for all we know. There's no way of catching who did this, is there?"

Miller sighed.

"No," he admitted. "We don't have much to go on here. I can start calling rental agencies, see if any black sedans have been rented in the last few days. But that's going to be like looking for a needle in a haystack."

He went on: "Either it was someone who followed you, or someone you know—who knows every detail of your regular routine."

"Someone who wants to kill me—or at least scare me to death."

He didn't have any reassurances for her. He turned into her neighborhood and parked on the street in front of her town house.

"My car," she said, as if only then remembering that she'd left it behind.

"I'm going to go down to the station and file an official report on this, so if you'll give me your keys, I'll get another officer and come back here tonight with your car," Miller offered. "If you've got an extra set of keys, I'll just lock it up and leave the keys inside your glove box, all right?"

Natalie nodded. "Thanks."

They dashed to the door through the rain, and she dug out her keys beneath the shelter of the small front porch. Her outside lights were off, and she turned toward the streetlight as she fished them out of her purse, then pivoted back around to unlock the door.

Switching on the lights as she went, she headed straight for the kitchen. Her little dog, sharp nails clattering on the tiled floor, scampered happily to greet her.

The dog wriggled its welcome in her arms when she picked her up.

"Prissy! Ow!" She nearly dropped the dog. As it was, the little animal landed almost headfirst, whining at the indignity.

Natalie held her hands palm up, the raw abrasions looking worse in the bright indoor light than they had in the parking lot.

"She scratched my palm where it's already cut. Poor baby. I didn't mean to drop you."

She knelt by the peach ball of dog and ran a comforting finger along the top of the animal's head.

Miller came closer, and Prissy scooted back.

"Let me see," he said, drawing Natalie back up and taking her hands into his. His eyes riveted to the ugly scrapes on her palms. Swearing, he pulled her toward the sink. "I knew we should have had someone look at this while we were at the hospital. Where do you keep your towels?" he asked, turning on the water, testing the temperature.

"Under there." She pointed to a deep drawer under one of the counters.

He pulled out a clean, soft dish towel and wet it in the running water. She set her purse on the counter, taking out the caller ID box she'd bought and setting it down. Miller took her hands again and began to gently dab at the wounds, cleaning them.

She winced, bit her lip, stinging pain radiating all the way up her arms as the shock that had nearly numbed her wore off.

As he worked, Miller kept his attention focused on the task. She closed her eyes, standing very still, breathing in his seductive male scent, fighting the painful desire to lay her head on his shoulder the way she could have done once.

Traitorous tears squeezed beneath her lids, and she felt too weak at the moment to stop them. She wasn't a crier, but tonight her defenses were shot.

He finished. "You're crying."

Her lashes flashed up.

"I hurt you," he breathed huskily. "Why didn't you say anything? I'm sorry."

The helpless guilt in his eyes tore at her ravaged heart.

"No— It's not that. It's—" She didn't know

how to finish. Her heart hurt a million times worse than her hands, but she couldn't tell him that.

How could she explain that his tenderness was killing her?

Everything seemed to be crashing down on her—all the fear, the pain, past and present, swirling together. Her knees felt incredibly wobbly. She leaned against the edge of the counter.

"I think I'm just having some kind of delayed stress reaction," she said, her thoughts disjointed as she drew her hands out of his. His eyes on her were watchful, dark, unreadable.

"You need to get changed out of those wet clothes," he said firmly. "Then you need a drink and bed. You have wine?"

She nodded numbly.

"Get changed," he said. "I'll get you a drink." He shooed her out.

The kitchen was larger, colder, when she was gone. Miller worked not to imagine Natalie upstairs, changing clothes in that flowery bower of a room. He busied himself with the job of hooking up her new caller ID box, then found a bottle of blush chablis in the refrigerator and poured a glass.

She came back, dressed in a big Texas wildflowers T-shirt and denim shorts, baring her scraped knees. Her eyes were huge, exhaustion pulling at her mouth. Yet still she looked remarkably pretty and warm and alive, standing there with her shiny, thick hair falling down around her shoulders.

"I hooked up your caller ID box," he told her.

He was going to have a hard time leaving her. She was in danger, and he wanted to stay with her, hold her and comfort her and make all sorts of other stupid mistakes that he would be sorry for later. Like finding out if the taste of her lips would be as familiar as the fit of her body in his arms had been.

And once he'd done that—once he'd kissed her—what then?

He'd want more.

"I can get your car back to you in a little while," he said as he handed her the glass of wine.

"Thank you," she said, taking it, her fingers brushing his in the exchange.

She took a sip.

"You have messages," he said, nodding at the phone answering machine on her counter. "Maybe there's one there from the perpetrator. Why don't you check before I leave? If you ever get a message from the person doing this to you, I can take it to the lab, have the voice analyzed. It won't help us much right now, but later, after we've got someone, we can use voice-matching to help nail them."

"Okay."

She punched the button on the machine. There were two messages from Brad Harrison.

"Natalie, where are you?" the first one played. "I'm worried. I called the office and Ginny told me about the box. You should be home from the hospital by now."

The second was briefer, asking her to call as soon as she got in. "I'm worried," he repeated.

The third message was from Justus Buchanan, ordering her to phone him ASAP.

Silence swelled between them after the tape automatically rewound.

Obviously, she had plenty of people to worry about her. She didn't need *him*.

Damn his foolish heart for the stupidity of wanting her to.

He moved out of the kitchen, toward the entry hall, and she followed. He reached the door and she touched him suddenly, stopping him.

"Wait," she said. She put the glass of wine down on the hall table.

He stood there, watching her. She felt tongue-tied and had to force herself to keep going.

"I—I want to thank you," she said.

"It's not necessary."

She lowered her eyes, and her long lashes cast shadows over her pale cheeks. "Okay, that's not really what I wanted to say."

He waited, watching her. She drew a breath, let it go, and raised her soft gaze to him.

"About before. About—" She blushed, but lifted her chin and kept on. "I wanted to say that I'm sorry. About everything. We were kids, but that's no excuse. I shouldn't have made an excuse at all. I'm just—I'm sorry. I wanted to say that."

His body went very still. There was some unfathomable pain in her eyes, something that seemed just beyond his comprehension.

Something secret. He was tempted to probe, to demand answers.

Would she give him her secrets?

The doorbell rang, and the unexpected chime made her draw in a sharp breath.

She raised her hand to her chest. "Nerves," she said, shaking her head. "I'm going to have a heart attack before this is finished, I swear."

After first checking the peephole, she flung the door open and he watched another man sweep her into his arms.

SEVEN

The man was tall, athletic, with a lean face and a strong chin. His T-shirt and shorts were casual but somehow meticulous at the same time. And he was holding on to Natalie.

Tension gripped Miller's stomach.

The guy was vaguely familiar. *Harrison,* he realized suddenly.

Brad Harrison.

Miller noticed the way Natalie's little dog came yapping happily up to Harrison, as if accustomed to seeing him.

"I've been worried about you," Brad said, his gaze raking Miller as Natalie stepped back slightly. She stayed by his side, his arm looped casually around her waist. "Did you get my messages? Ginny told me—"

"Yes, I'm sorry! I just got home and checked my machine." She extended her hand, indicating Miller. "Brad, you remember Miller Brannigan."

Miller held out his hand. "Nice to see you again, Brad."

Brad's expression shifted from startled to wary.

He moved his arm away from Natalie in order to shake Miller's hand.

"Brannigan," he said by way of greeting, then gave Natalie a questioning glance.

"Miller's the officer who's been handling my case," she explained, and gave Brad a brief summary of what had happened at the hospital.

"My God!" Brad exclaimed when she finished. "You could have been killed." He turned to Miller and gave him a hard look. "Have you got any leads?"

"We don't have anything solid so far."

Brad's mouth thinned.

"Great. Natalie's had her house ransacked, received threatening phone calls, and had that grisly delivery at her office. Now she's nearly been run down. And the police have no leads."

"We're doing everything we can," Miller said, his tone deceptively mild in consideration of the irritation pumping through his bloodstream.

Natalie tensed visibly.

"Brad, stop it," she said quickly. "Miller's worked very hard on my case."

Brad stared at her for a contemplative second, then sighed.

"I'm just worried about you." He looked at Miller. "Didn't mean to snap at you, Miller." Still, his body posture issued a subtle challenge as he went on. "It was good of you to bring her home, but I can take it from here on out."

"I was just leaving." Miller moved to the door without further comment.

Natalie followed him onto the porch, flipping on the outside light. She picked up the extra set of keys to her car on the way out.

"Thank you again," she said, handing him the keys. "I know you're doing everything you can."

She gave him a tremulous smile, and a wanting, sharp and deep, nearly brought him to his knees. He didn't want to leave her. He felt an almost primitive need to be the one to protect Natalie.

He wanted, needed, to hate her. Why couldn't he? *Because she seemed like the gentle, innocent girl he'd thought he'd known, right up until that last day.*

Frustration chewed at his already edgy nerves. Was he being taken in again? He'd believed Natalie was a sweet, pure-hearted girl all those years ago—and he'd been completely wrong.

Now was he letting her suck him right back in with just a bat of her beautiful green eyes. He couldn't let it happen.

"Stop thanking me," he clipped out harshly. "It's my job."

He left her standing there. The rain had stopped again, and he took off across the wet yard, not bothering to follow the path of the sidewalk. A shiny silver Lexus, which he assumed belonged to Brad Harrison, was parked in the driveway.

He scowled as he sat down in his own car. Natalie had gone back inside, shut the door. She was safe in the company of her friend. He should be happy about that, relieved.

So what the hell was bothering him?

Nothing romantic was how she'd characterized her relationship with Brad. Yet there was something possessive about Brad's attitude toward Natalie.

Or was *he* the one who was possessive?

"You didn't have to be rude to him." Natalie walked past Brad and sat down on the couch in the living room. She crossed her arms and stared at him.

Brad followed her, slipping down beside her.

"I'm just worried about you, and what are the police doing to protect you?"

"Everything they can," she replied, then sighed, pressing her hand to her forehead and closing her eyes. She was feeling tired and testy and completely incapable of dealing with one more iota of stress. "Don't make me mad at you. I'm not up to it."

"I'm sorry," he apologized immediately. "You're terrified, and on top of that I know seeing Miller must have hurt. Why didn't you tell me he was the officer handling this case?"

"I didn't want to talk about it," she admitted, her heart softening as she leaned over and rested her head on his shoulder.

She couldn't stay mad. She was too exhausted, and Brad was too good a friend. He was protective of her, and she could hardly fault him for that, especially now.

Her eyes still closed, she could almost imagine it was Miller's shoulder instead.

Her lashes flashed up. She had to stop thinking this way. She *had* to, or she'd go stark, raving mad.

She moved away, straightened.

"It was hard seeing him, wasn't it?" Brad asked quietly. "I know it had to be. That's why I was so impatient with him, I guess. Having to deal with Miller Brannigan along with everything else—it's just too much for you, Natalie. You shouldn't have to do that right now. You want me to call the police station tomorrow and see about having another officer assigned to handle the investigation?"

Natalie blinked, straightened.

"No, don't do that."

Brad seemed taken aback.

"Why not?"

"Because—" She scrambled for an answer that made sense, an answer that didn't come from the deeply secret place in her heart that still yearned for Miller. "Because he's good at his job. Very good. I can handle it. And if I did want him removed from the case, I would call the station myself—you know that. I know that you only want to take care of me, but I don't need you to. I can take of myself."

"I know. You're so independent. But I'm scared for you right now."

"I'm being careful, believe me." She sighed and stared blindly at the curtained window. "Miller's turned into a really fine person—you know that? I always knew that he would."

The room was silent for several beats.

"Natalie, sweetheart, don't torture yourself." Brad reached his arm around her, squeezed her shoulder. "Come on. Look at you. Have you been sleeping? You look like hell."

Her lips twisted in a wry expression. She turned and looked at him.

"Oh, Brad, you're such a flatterer."

He laughed, hugged her close into his shoulder. "You know I think you're gorgeous."

Natalie had to smile.

"Yeah, yeah." Brad had seen her at her absolute worst ten years ago, and he'd told her that she was beautiful every step of the way during that long, awful year when she'd been in and out of treatment in the cancer ward of a Houston hospital.

She'd nearly died, and still Brad had told her she was beautiful.

"You know you lost your credibility on that one," she teased.

"Hey, I mean it," he said. "You're adorable. I love you. And I'm scared to death for you." His expression sobered. "What are we going to do about this? Start from the beginning, go over everything that's happened, everything the police have done."

Pulling away from him, Natalie drew up her legs, curling into the corner of the couch. He watched her, listening carefully, interjecting questions and comments.

When she was through, he told her what he thought about the situation.

"Nobody you know would do this. Ethan and Ginny may have their problems, but it's just crazy to think either one of them would do this to you. It's insane. And if any of your father's employees were angry with him, they'd take it out on him, not you. This sounds like the work of a stalker, a psycho. Someone's targeted you. There's a nutcase on every corner, you know."

"Well, now I feel better."

Brad regarded her seriously. "It's the truth, sweetheart."

"So what am I supposed to do? I'm not moving in with my father. I think I'd rather let somebody kill me," she joked blackly. "Which reminds me, he left a message. I need to phone him."

Brad got up, too.

"I think I should spend the night on your couch," he offered. "You shouldn't be alone."

"Don't be silly."

He drew his brows together in a frown.

"If I go home," he said, "and something happened to you, I would never forgive myself, Natalie. Let me stay."

"No." She was tempted to let him stay, but she hated letting whoever was threatening her take over her life. "I have the best security system money can buy—you know that. Sound and motion sensors, the works. It's Fort Knox here, okay? Go home."

Brad was silent for a few seconds. "All right," he gave in reluctantly. He stared her straight in the eye. "But if anything happens, anything at all, you call me and I'll be here. Right?"

"Right." She tipped up on her toes and kissed him on the cheek. "I promise."

When he was gone, she set her security system and then dialed her father's number. He wanted her to come home, of course, and her nerves were aching with tension by the time she hung up. No way could she handle going back to his house in her current state of stress, and dealing with his suffocating domination.

The more distance she maintained between herself and her father, the better. No matter how alone she felt in her own home, she knew too well how much more alone she would feel in her father's house.

The sad part was, she was almost certain he was lonely, too. But somehow, the two of them were only more lonely when they were together—not less.

She peeked out the front window and saw that Miller had delivered her car to her driveway. He hadn't come in, and she wished he had.

Stupid, she berated herself. Stupid, stupid, and more stupid.

Upstairs, she changed into a nightshirt and, with Prissy curled up on her pillow at the foot of the bed, she turned off the light. In the darkness, the only sounds her own breaths and Prissy's sleepy groans, she worked to release the tension in her muscles.

She willed herself to breathe deeply, evenly. Her side was sore from her fall in the hospital parking lot, and her hands ached dully.

And she was scared. There was someone out there, somewhere, who wanted to hurt her. In the blackness of her bedroom, her skin crawled.

Natalie sat straight up, gasping, her heart banging against the wall of her chest. A loud siren slashed through the house, reverberating in her head. Terror fired through her bloodstream.

Her security alarm!

"Oh, my God."

Was someone in the house?

Lunging out of bed, she ran to the door of her bedroom, slamming it shut and locking it. Adrenaline raced through her system.

She punched in the code on the lighted security system keypad to the left of her bedroom door and the house went dead silent. As her eyes adjusted to the darkness, she dashed to the telephone on her nightstand. She pulled it down with her to the carpeted floor, where she huddled and dialed 911, her heart pounding in her ears so loud that she wondered if she'd be able to hear the emergency operator's voice.

Prissy whimpered beneath the bed, didn't even come out when Natalie held out her hand to her.

The dispatcher came on the line.

"My alarm went off," she blurted out. "I'm afraid someone is in my house."

Her own voice was barely recognizable to herself, it shook so much.

"Ma'am, we'll have someone right there." The dispatcher reeled off her address in a calm voice. "Is that correct?"

"Yes."

"Tell me where you are in the house."

"Upstairs. My bedroom."

The conversation was eerily familiar. Her head spun and her stomach pitched.

When would this stop?

The dispatcher asked questions, and she answered. Her gaze fell on the glowing digital numbers on the clock radio atop her nightstand. Twelve-thirty A.M. The last time she'd looked at her clock before she'd fallen asleep, it had been eleven forty-five.

She'd barely gotten any rest—for two nights running. The nonstop fatigue made her nauseous on top of everything else.

Pounding from below and a shout of "Police!" came as such a stunning relief, she couldn't speak for several seconds.

"They're here," she told the dispatcher.

She hung up and flew downstairs, flipping on the light in the hall as she went.

The sight of two burly officers beyond her peephole made her feel even better. She unlocked the door and pulled it open. The officers commenced an immediate examination of the town house.

"Ma'am," one of them called from the laundry room near the back door.

He pointed at the window.

"Somebody broke your window out," he said. "Must have set off your sound sensors." He shrugged. "Maybe the alarm scared him off. He didn't even try to raise the window. We'll check around outside, but my bet's that he's long gone."

Natalie stared at the window. Broken shards of glass littered the tiled floor of her tiny laundry room. The window was small, but even a good-sized man could squeeze through it once it was opened. Hysteria clawed up her throat.

She closed her eyes for a second, fighting it. Whoever had done this might be gone now, but she had a horrible feeling they'd be back. She *knew* they'd be back.

What she didn't know was when.

"Ma'am, are you all right? Is there someone you want to call? You probably don't want to be alone here tonight with this broken window."

She took a deep breath, opened her eyes. *Is there someone you want to call?*

"Yes."

She needed to feel safe, if only for a few hours. And in a world suddenly gone mad, it was just part of the madness that the one person who could make her feel that way was Miller.

EIGHT

"Don't feel as if you have to stay." Natalie stood in her open front doorway. She could see the police cruiser pulling away on the rain-slick street beyond Miller and snuggled her robe closer around her in the chilly dampness of the night.

Arriving within minutes following her call, Miller had given her just enough time to start regretting the automatic impulse that had made her turn to him for support. After asking her if she was all right, he'd efficiently assessed the situation—inspecting the broken window in the laundry room and talking with the two police officers who had responded to her 911 call. He'd walked with them out to their cruiser.

Now he'd come back to the small porch in front of her town house, turning his attention directly on her for the first time since right after his arrival. He was dressed in those worn jeans that reminded her what a killer body he had.

She didn't know if he slept in them, or if he'd just yanked them on when she'd called. His plain T-shirt and light leather jacket reminded her that she was garbed in her robe. She hadn't been uncomfortable in it around the officers who were total strangers to her.

After all, she supposed police officers must be accustomed to dealing with people who'd been roused by crime in the middle of the night and were in all states of dress and undress.

But she was uncomfortable around Miller, even though the robe was very modest, long and thick, covering her completely.

It was the second night in a row that he'd come to her house, the second night in a row she'd had to stand before him in her robe. Maybe she should start dressing for work before she went to bed.

A hysterical bubble of laughter ached in her chest at the bizarre thought.

She looked at Miller, focused on the situation at hand. "I shouldn't have called you. I'm sorry."

"I don't mind staying," Miller said, pushing his fingertips into his jacket pockets.

"I don't want to impose on you. I shouldn't have called you in the first place."

Miller stepped a few inches closer, his eyes on her. "But you did call me."

"I was having a weak moment," she said honestly, then wished the words back right away. What did she think she was doing? This wasn't the time to start being honest with Miller.

That ship had sailed a long time ago—and she hadn't been on it.

"A weak moment?" he said, and stepped closer

until he was standing right in front of her. "What do you mean by that?"

She was definitely having a weak moment now, and getting weaker all the time. Miller affected her in a way no other man ever had. She'd thought all these years that perhaps her eighteen-year-old mind had dreamed up Miller's stunning impact on her senses.

She'd been wrong.

It was real, too real. She was like a teenager with raging hormones all over again—only she was twenty-eight years old and she should know better. She *did* know better. But she couldn't change the way she felt.

He was waiting for her to respond.

"I don't mean anything by that," she said. "I just . . . I just knew that you would make me feel safe. You seem very . . . competent."

She flushed. It didn't seem as if she could say anything in this conversation that wasn't completely humiliating, but she couldn't figure a way out of it, so she stared at the floor of the porch. She focused on a jagged crack in the porch pavement in front of Miller's boots as if she thought the right thing to say or do would magically appear there.

It didn't.

What did appear were Miller's strong fingers, reaching out to lift her chin with gentle pressure, forcing her to face him. The touch of his warm fingers all but burned her skin, she was that ultra-aware of it.

"Then why do you look so scared?" he asked in a quiet, husky voice that seemed intimate suddenly.

Here, with the empty street beyond them, in the buttery luminescence of the porchlight, it seemed as if they might be the only living humans for miles around in spite of the obvious fact that inside the town homes surrounding them there were bound to be dozens and dozens of people. Yet at this moment her porch felt as intimate as the most remote island in the tropics.

Miller was right, of course: She was scared. Scared of being alone with him like this and, at the same time, scared he'd leave.

Scared she'd never be alone with him again.

The answer to his question was elusive and complicated, so elusive and complicated that even she didn't know the full answer, and she couldn't possibly express that confusion to Miller.

It was too intangible and emotional . . . and much, much too private.

"I just feel terrible about disturbing your night," she told him.

"I wouldn't feel right leaving you here alone under the circumstances. I can bunk on your couch, or you can call someone else to come over here. Or you can go somewhere else for the night. But I'm already awake and here, so it might as well be me," he pointed out reasonably.

There was an awkward silence that Natalie didn't know how to fill.

"I can camp out in my car, you know," he said. "I don't have to come in."

"I'm not letting you camp out in your car," she said immediately, then realized with embarrassment that she'd made him wait outside all this time in the damp chill. "Come in. I can't believe I've been making you stand out here on the porch."

She stood back and gave Miller room to pass by her into the town house, then shut the door behind him, locking it promptly with fingers that shook more than they should have. More than could be explained by the now past adrenaline rush of the broken window incident.

It was Miller who had her body trembling, her voice quavering. Baby-sitting her here tonight was way beyond Miller's job description.

Why was he doing it?

Just thinking about that was upsetting. She didn't need to start hoping that there was a chance Miller was taking this case to a personal level.

It would kill her all over again to hope—and have her hopes dashed.

What she and Miller had shared was gone, kaput, terminated, never coming back. Why was she having such a hard time with such a simple fact?

She was just someone he'd once known, someone he'd once loved, and that made an already dedicated officer feel an even greater obligation to his duty. But that was all it was: duty.

Wasn't it?

"I don't have a guest bedroom," she said.

"The couch'll do."

She felt so awkward, she wanted to shrivel right into the woodwork. Even ten years ago, they'd never shared an entire night in the same house. They'd wanted to, had dreamed of it, talked of it, made wild and completely unworkable plans for how to make it happen. But of course it never had.

Her father had been disapproving enough of her relationship with Miller. It was rebellion enough that she'd even dared to date him.

Natalie jerked her thoughts from the painful, traitorous path they'd taken. Memories were seductive. Dangerous.

"Okay. Uh, well, I'll find an extra pillow and a blanket for you," she said.

She hustled off without giving Miller a chance to say he didn't need anything. She needed something to do, something with which to busy herself.

There was an extra pillow in the linen closet upstairs. She found a pillowcase for it and a light coverlet, and returned to the living room. Miller sat on the couch, his long legs slung casually in front of him. He stood when she came in.

He inclined his head.

"Thanks."

"I hope you'll be comfortable. Do you need anything else?"

"I'll be fine."

Miller was watching her intently. Her heart drummed against the wall of her chest. Could he see her thoughts, see how punishingly aware of him she was? Was he aware of her, too?

She was being ridiculous. She was losing it, totally losing it. Her life was in danger, and she was obsessing over a long-lost love.

Knowledge of her own idiocy didn't do anything to ease her fluttering stomach.

"I'm going to bed," she said flatly, irritated with herself.

"Good night," he said.

He looked so good, so strong and big. The leathery scent of his jacket clung to him, mixing with his musky maleness. A pang of desperate longing sheared through her body.

She tried not to look like she was running away when she headed for the stairs.

Miller stared blindly at the ceiling overhead. Natalie's drapes were too thick to let in even the thinnest slice of moonlight between the slats in the blinds that covered the windows.

He couldn't stop being aware of Natalie upstairs, his body tingling at the pulse points and keeping him awake. It was crazy. It couldn't have been more obvious that she was uncomfortable around him, that she couldn't wait to get away from him.

If his ego were more fragile, he might be insulted. As it was, he had to admit to disappointment—which was irrational.

What had he expected, that she'd invite him up to her bed, the better to protect her?

He almost laughed, but rolled his eyes in the darkness instead, battling the dark levity with frustrated disgust at his own inability to separate Natalie—and their past together—from his reaction to the current situation. His past with Natalie was unshakably intertwined with the present, whether he wanted it to be or not.

If not for the past, he wouldn't be taking her case so personally. He wouldn't be here now to watch over her. He wouldn't sense every breath she took upstairs even though he couldn't actually hear her.

He didn't want to think he still had tender feelings for Natalie. Anger was the only feeling he allowed himself in connection with her.

But the more time he spent with her, the harder it was to maintain that anger. And the harder it was to keep believing she was shallow and heartless. But if she wasn't shallow and heartless, what did that mean about that awful day she'd walked away?

A noise drew his attention.

His body hummed to instant alert. It was a breath, a footfall, a creak of sound from the kitchen accompanied by a sliver of light shafting outward through the open archway connecting the first-floor rooms.

The shaft of light drew him.

He didn't have to check out the noise. He knew without a doubt that it was Natalie, rummaging around in her own kitchen. Nothing dangerous about that.

Except for the danger to his own heart if he couldn't stay away from her. And, quite simply, he could not. So he went to her, because he had no choice, because something inside him needed to see her, breathe her, be with her now while he had the chance.

He was a full-blown idiot.

She stood with the refrigerator door open, her robe gaping, the light from the appliance revealing the Texas wildflowers nightshirt and her creamy bare thighs and calves.

Seeming instantly aware of him, she gasped and jerked upright, dropping the half-gallon jug of milk in her hand. Fortunately it was plastic and not full, so it resulted only in a sloshy thud as it hit the floor.

He could see the petrified look in her huge eyes just before it morphed into relief—then something more difficult to read—when she realized it was him. She took a steadying breath.

"I didn't mean to startle you," he said.

He knelt to pick up the milk jug, handing it to her as he straightened.

"Thanks." She tucked the milk jug in the crook of her arm. "I guess I startle pretty easily lately. I hope I didn't wake you up. I couldn't sleep."

"I wasn't sleeping, either." He wondered if she'd been upstairs, aware of him the way he'd been downstairs aware of her.

Her scent teased him. It was flowery, though he

couldn't place it specifically. He didn't know anything about flowers or women's perfumes.

He just knew that Natalie looked so soft in the light and shadows, and so absolutely, stunningly beautiful. His heart crashed inside his chest.

"I came down here for some cookies and milk," she said. "Comfort food."

He noticed the careful way she held the jug of milk in her fingertips, not letting it rub against her palms, and he remembered the injury to her hands.

"Are your hands bothering you?"

She shrugged, trying to pull her robe together at the same time she was holding on to the milk jug and the refrigerator door.

"They're stinging," she admitted.

"Give me that." Miller took the milk from her and told himself that it was pretty ludicrous to be feeling disappointed to discover that what kept her awake was physical discomfort, not contemplations of him.

It would probably give her a good laugh if she could read his thoughts.

Natalie shut the refrigerator door, bathing them in darkness for a second before she made her way by touch to switch on the light.

"I could do it myself," she argued when he started opening cabinets.

"Where do you keep your glasses?"

"There." She pointed. "It's not necessary for you to treat me like an invalid," she protested. "I'm quite sure I could pour a glass of milk."

"Anyone ever tell you it's hard to do you a favor?" Miller asked, pulling down two glasses and setting them on the counter.

She gave up and went to the pantry. "No," she said, shutting the pantry door, coming back with a box of chocolate chip cookies.

Miller gave her a look.

"Well, maybe," she admitted. "Okay, once or twice. I like my independence. What's wrong with that?"

Even now, at this late hour, barefoot and in her robe, she managed to exude a fragile self-possession that was both admirable and frustrating. But he could see anxiety, exhaustion . . . and fear in her eyes that belied her careful shell.

She wouldn't admit to that truth easily, he suspected. But that truth remained nonetheless, and made it only that much more difficult for him to guard his rebel heart against her.

"Nothing's wrong with being independent," he conceded. "As long as you realize that leaning on someone every once in a while doesn't make you weak."

"I know that," she said, prickly.

Her slender shoulders were stiff and she sounded defensive.

"Glad to hear it," he commented, pouring the milk as he spoke.

"I don't mean to seem ungrateful," she said hurriedly. "I appreciate your help, everything you've done."

He set the jug down.

"It's just hard for you to accept it," he said, leveling his gaze on her. "Especially from me."

She stood there, her eyes full of those haunting secret thoughts that he could never read. He wanted to shake her, make her tell him everything she was thinking.

But he had no right.

"Yes," she admitted. "Of course. This is . . . awkward. Isn't it? I mean, what are we doing here, having cookies and milk together after all these years? It doesn't make sense."

The vulnerable little hitch in her soft voice gave his heart another lurch. Her questions sought confirmation of his private thoughts, and revealed a little of her own.

Perhaps she wasn't so immune to him as she tried to seem. But what *did* she feel? The truth was locked up with all her other secrets.

He reminded himself that when this investigation was closed, they would go their separate ways again. He had to put a tight lid on these feelings, these tender, hungry feelings that twined together with the bitterness. They had no place in the here and now of his relationship with Natalie.

"I don't know what we're doing," he admitted. "I just know that I couldn't live with myself if I left you here alone tonight."

"This isn't part of your job," she pointed out. "You don't have to be here, you don't have to do this."

He nodded tensely. "You're right."

Heartbeats passed.

"Then why are you?" Her voice was no louder than a breath.

Every inch of him yearned, ached, to hold her. It was all he could do to restrain himself from taking her into his arms.

He didn't have the strength to lie, too.

"Because I care about what happens to you," he said. "Because I want to know that you're safe tonight." There was more, and he made himself say it. He needed to stop trying to hold on to the bitterness. Whatever the truth was about that long-ago spring, maybe he could move on, break the invisible bond between them, if he let the anger go. "And because you were right about what you said before. We were kids, and kids make mistakes. I know I made plenty of my own in those days."

He had no right to punish her for not loving him enough. And wasn't that what he'd really been doing? Punishing her for not loving him with the same unending passion with which he had loved her?

She stared at him with huge, luminous eyes that he could drown in.

"Thank you."

"We have a history together," he said, "but it's the present we have to deal with now, not the past. I'm not here to make you uncomfortable, to make you feel guilty for anything."

The clock ticked on the wall. Outside, darkness pressed in against the windows. She'd forgotten to pull the blind over the kitchen sink, and the inky black outside reminded him that other people were snuggled together in their beds.

He wondered what it would feel like to snuggle in bed with Natalie. They'd never made love on a bed, hadn't had that luxury in their furtive teenage couplings. They'd made love on a blanket in the woods behind the high school stadium.

He shook off the provocative swirl of remembrances that threatened to suck him in.

"Are we going to stand here all night, or are we going to eat some cookies?" he asked briskly.

Natalie let out a surprised laugh.

"I guess we're going to eat some cookies," she said finally.

They ended up watching the sci-fi B-movie classics marathon on one of the cable stations. They sat on the couch, munching cookies and drinking glasses of cold milk while a monster blob took over a Midwestern city in crackly black-and-white on the screen.

It was intimate, yet completely proper at the same time. They didn't talk for a long time, long past the point when they both had finished snacking and drained their glasses of milk.

Natalie sank into the soft couch pillows. Despite his determination to maintain what professional distance he had left at this point, he found himself studying her. Her fatigue was evident in her drawn face, yet she seemed to be resisting sleep.

He touched her arm.

"Natalie, go to bed."

"I'm fine." She looked at him. "Oh, I'm keeping you up."

He shook his head.

"No, I'm fine." He was accustomed—much more than she, he was sure—to staying up all night. He still occasionally pulled a relief shift on patrol overnight. His body adjusted to lack of sleep with practiced automation. "But you look as if you could fall asleep sitting up. Go to bed."

She stared at him, the violet smears of fatigue under her eyes evident even in the flickering TV light. Her next words were simple and soft, but so strong that they tore straight to his heart, devastating his barriers and all his fine promises of moving on.

"I don't want to be alone."

NINE

"You're not alone," he said. "I'm here."

The tiny flame of hope, hope she'd tried so hard not to hold on to, fanned to life inside her. Fanned to life over something as tenuous as the light of concern in Miller's eyes.

She was so pathetic.

"I'm a little jumpy about going upstairs," she said, struggling to pull herself together before she did something stupid. "It's silly. I'm just stressed out."

She didn't know how to deal with her feelings for Miller—with this awful, hopeless hope—but she knew what to do about her fear of going upstairs. She should just *do it.* Miller wasn't going to be coming over to baby-sit her every night.

"If going upstairs is bothering you, it's not silly," he said. He hit the mute button on the remote, then placed it back on the coffee table. "And stress is not something to ignore, especially if it's keeping you from sleeping."

He was watching her intently. The flickering light played over his chiseled features, reflecting

THE PUBLISHERS OF ZEBRA BOUQUET

are making this special offer to lovers of contemporary romances to introduce this exciting new line of novels. Zebra's Bouquet Romances have been praised by critics and authors alike as being of the highest quality and best written romantic fiction available today.

♥

EACH FULL-LENGTH NOVEL

has been written by authors you know and love as well as by up and coming writers that you'll only find with Zebra Bouquet. We'll bring you the newest novels by world famous authors like Vanessa Grant, Judy Gill, Ann Josephson and award winning Suzanne Barrett and Leigh Greenwood—to name just a few. Zebra Bouquet's editors have selected only the very best and highest quality for publication under the Bouquet banner.

♥

YOU'LL BE TREATED

to glamorous settings from Carnavale in Rio, the moneyed high-powered offices of New York's Wall Street, the rugged north coast of British Columbia, and the mountains of North Carolina. Bouquet Romances use these settings to spin tales of star-crossed lovers that are sure to captivate you. These stories will keep you enthralled to the very happy end.

♥

4 FREE NOVELS
As a way to introduce you to these terrific romances, the publishers of Bouquet are offering Zebra Romance readers Four Free Bouquet novels. They are yours for the asking with no obligation to buy a single book. Read them at your leisure. We are sure that after you've read these introductory books you'll want more! (If you do not wish to receive any further Bouquet novels, simply write "cancel" on the invoice and return to us within 10 days.)

SAVE 20% WITH HOME DELIVERY
Each month you'll receive four just published Bouquet Romances. We'll ship them to you as soon as they are printed (you may even get them before the bookstores). You'll have 10 days to preview these exciting novels for Free. If you decide to keep them, you'll be billed the special preferred home subscription price of just $3.20 per book; a total of just $12.80 — that's a savings of 20% off the publisher's price. If for any reason you are not satisfied simply return the novels for full credit, no questions asked. You'll never have to purchase a minimum number of books and you may cancel your subscription at any time.

GET STARTED TODAY –
NO RISK AND NO OBLIGATION

To get your introductory gift of 4 Free Bouquet Romances fill out and mail the enclosed Free Book Certificate today. We'll ship your free selections as soon as we receive this information. Remember that you are under no obligation. This is a risk free offer from the publishers of Zebra Bouquet Romances.

FREE BOOK CERTIFICATE

Yes! I would like to take you up on your offer. Please send me 4 Free Bouquet Romance Novels as my introductory gift. I understand that unless I tell you otherwise, I will then receive the 4 newest Bouquet novels to preview each month Free for 10 days. If I decide to keep them I'll pay the preferred home subscriber's price of just $3.20 each (a total of only $12.80) plus $1.50 for shipping and handling. That's a 20% savings off the publisher's price. I understand that I may return any shipment for full credit no questions asked and I may cancel this subscription at any time with no obligation. Regardless of what I decide to do, the 4 Free introductory novels are mine to keep as Bouquet's gift.

Name _____

Address _____ Apt. _____

City _____ State ____ Zip _____

Telephone ( ) _____

Signature _____ BN129A

(If under 18, parent or guardian must sign.)

For your convenience you may charge your shipments automatically to a Visa or MasterCard so you'll never have to worry about late payments and missing shipments. If you return any shipment we'll credit your account.

Yes, charge my credit card for my "Bouquet Romance" shipments until I tell you otherwise.
☐ Visa ☐ MasterCard

Account Number _____

Expiration Date _____

Signature _____

Orders subject to acceptance by Zebra Home Subscription Service. Terms and Prices subject to change. Offer valid in U.S. only.

If this response card is missing,
call us at 1-888-345-BOOK.

Be sure to visit our website at
www.kensingtonbooks.com

BOUQUET ROMANCE
120 Brighton Road
P.O. BOX 5214
Clifton, New Jersey 07015-5214

AFFIX
STAMP
HERE

in his impossibly blue eyes. She wished so hard that she knew what he was thinking.

She swallowed thickly.

"I'll manage," she said. "Sleep's overrated, anyway."

"You don't have to go up there yet," he suggested quietly. "They give us a lot of training in stress relief at the department. Trust me, cops know stress. If you want, I could teach you a few relaxation techniques."

She couldn't imagine relaxing around Miller. He made her feel tight and hot inside. Nope, not relaxed, not at all.

"I don't know. I don't think I'm too good a student at relaxation." She couldn't believe the thin, whispery voice was her own, but it was.

"Just give it a try." His low voice was nothing but a whisper in the night, too. He shifted closer, touched her shoulder to turn her slightly on the couch.

She should go upstairs. Now.

But his incredible fingers were touching her, brushing the hair off her neck, leaving tingling heat in their wake. And she was oh so weak.

She could feel his breath at her nape. His magic fingers started massaging her tense muscles.

"Close your eyes," he said quietly, still rubbing her neck.

The feel of his hands was bliss and torment at the same time. She squeezed her eyes shut.

"Concentrate on your breathing. Take slow, deep breaths. Now, I want you to progressively relax every part of your body. Tense your toes; then relax them."

"Tense them?"

"Yes, first tense them; then let go. Do it two or three times. Don't think about it. Just feel."

Dangerous advice. But oh how Natalie wanted only to feel. Thinking hurt so much sometimes.

She tensed her toes and relaxed them, repeating the process obediently.

"Now your feet," he instructed in a soothing voice, his arms sliding down around her, enfolding her gently, lightly, cushioning her. "Your legs."

Her limbs started feeling boneless. It occurred to her that she was liking this way too much; then she reminded herself that she wasn't allowed to think.

"Your arms."

His voice was so husky and sexy. She let herself feel the music of it, let its intoxicating measure fill her heart.

She felt herself smiling because the sound of Miller's voice made her so happy, and she didn't let herself think about how silly that was.

When he told her to relax her neck, she actually began to feel a little bit as if she were floating. She leaned her head back—because she wasn't thinking, just feeling.

She sighed, and snuggled, shifting just so, to be more comfortable. She was aware of an amazing lack of tension that she hadn't experienced in so long, she almost hadn't recognized the sensation. She felt so good.

He felt so good—next to her, touching her.

Opening her eyes, she looked into Miller's, realizing without knowing it that she'd cuddled right into the crook of his shoulder. Surprised, she lifted her head, but that only brought them closer. Nose to nose, mouth to mouth. A heartbeat apart.

She didn't think, didn't let herself think. Instead, she crossed a line, a line she knew he would never take the initiative to cross himself without a clear directive from her—if indeed he wanted to cross it at all.

A line she wouldn't cross, either, if she let herself think.

Acting on instinct, she moved that one heartbeat closer, shifting her body toward him at the same time. She heard him whisper her name and groan; then he was there, his lips brushing hers, exploring and tender. She was delirious with painful pleasure, dizzy with desperate need, shamelessly wanting so much more.

The kiss was cautious, as if he was afraid she'd rebuff him. But she looped her arms around his neck, deliberately encouraging him to deepen the kiss. And he did, a tormented sound coming from his throat as he suddenly tangled his fingers through her long hair and drew her tight.

Without a thought to the consequences, she threw herself into the moment as if she were still that young, naive girl who had loved the boy he had been with unchecked passion. She knew his kiss, would have known it if she'd been blindfolded.

And yet it was also different, more confident, more fierce.

He wasn't a boy now. He was a man.

Heat flooded her as he unleashed a hunger that matched her own. Her bones dissolved and she was helpless, holding on to him for dear life, praying he wouldn't ever let go.

And for a moment, a precious moment, despair and heartache didn't matter. Only this mattered, only Miller's arms and his kisses.

To Miller, Natalie tasted like a thousand lost days. She was so warm and sweet and alive, and she was in his arms with little mewls coming from her throat. He was delirious with needing her.

He was seconds away from a complete sensual meltdown. Natalie wanted him as much as he wanted her. His wildest fantasy was right here in his arms.

Would she be in his arms if she wasn't scared half out of her mind tonight?

He froze, and Natalie knew instantly that something had changed. That one of them had come to their senses—and it hadn't been her.

"Natalie," he said raggedly.

He pushed her away gently and she stared at him, shocked. Her breasts rose and fell rapidly.

"You don't know what you're doing," he said

roughly, before she could say anything. "Hell, I'm not sure I do, either. We can't do this."

She blinked, horrified—by what they'd done, by what she'd *wanted* to do, by her incredible loss of control.

And she *still* felt out of control. She *still* wanted to be back in his arms. She wanted that moment with no thinking, just feeling.

That moment had been heaven.

But it was gone, and everything was worse in the aftermath. She'd had a taste of what it was like to be in Miller's arms. He was more than a memory now. He was real, and he'd been hers— even if just for a moment.

She'd been content with her life, and now she wasn't, wouldn't be. Now she knew what she was missing.

Miller sat on the edge of the couch, turning away from her, scraping his hands through his hair. "God, when I look at you, I feel like I'm in high school again, with more hormones than brain cells. But I'm not in high school. I'm a cop, and I should be thinking more clearly than this." He looked back at her. "The way I see it, we've got more than enough to focus on with figuring out who's behind these incidents, and stopping them. Things are complicated enough without—"

He didn't finish the sentence.

The ice machine in her refrigerator cycled on automatically, generating a load of cubes into the icemaker. The noise from the kitchen filled the taut silence in the living room.

She looked away, touched a trembling finger to her mouth. Her lips felt tingly. Kissed. She felt shaky all over.

"I guess you make me feel as if I'm eighteen, too." She kept her face averted. She might be devastated, but he didn't have to know that. "We got a little carried away—that's all. Please don't feel bad about it."

The silence was heartrending.

There was only one thing left to say. She stood. "I'd better go upstairs."

Miller wanted to stop her, take her back into his arms, reclaim the precious moment when she'd been his again. But it wasn't possible. She wasn't his, hadn't really ever been.

She was in trouble, and he'd taken advantage of her despite his best intentions not to do so. He'd wanted her so much, too much.

And he'd nearly taken what he wanted, even knowing that there was a strong likelihood that *she* didn't know what she wanted.

To her, he was nothing more than safety in a world that had turned upside down. She was frightened, and he'd burned for her so violently that he'd betrayed the trust she'd placed in him.

He'd let himself be sucked into the powerful strength of their physical connection. And that was all it was: physical. It couldn't be more. They'd had their chance to see if there was more for the two of them, and there hadn't been. She'd made that decision. She needed him now, but it was for all the wrong reasons—and mixing it with sex would be a big mistake. Even a kiss was too much.

He had to be sure it didn't happen again.

TEN

Natalie arrived just as Miller's crime survival training class was starting on Saturday morning, sliding into the last seat in the back row. He stood at the front of the room, in snug jeans that showed off his long legs to perfection and a short-sleeved knit shirt stretched over his formidable broad shoulders.

Her heart gave a wrench when his gaze connected with hers. He nodded an acknowledgment as he carried on with his introductory notes.

She'd known what seeing him again would do to her—and so the strange, unbearable twisting inside her came as no surprise. For the last two nights—the night he'd spent on her couch, and the next—she'd lain awake with the very same feeling.

He'd left early on that morning after their kiss. She'd never gotten any sleep, though she hadn't told him that.

At dawn she'd come downstairs and found him up as well. He'd refused her offer of breakfast.

Even refused coffee, saying he had to get back to his apartment, get changed for work.

His rush to get away had been horrible—and a relief—at the same time.

She'd arranged to have the window fixed early in the day, and had made it into work by mid-morning. Ginny had called in sick, and Natalie was grateful not to have to face her friend's too perceptive eyes. She'd spent the rest of the day buried in a program analysis for a children's charity.

Brad had called, but like Ginny, Brad knew her too well, could see into her secret thoughts too easily, and she hadn't taken the call. Feeling guilty for ducking his concern, she'd tried to get in touch with him after she got home but had only gotten his machine.

There had been no word from Miller, and no more frightening incidents. She knew if he'd uncovered anything in the investigation into the box, or about the attack in the parking lot, he would have contacted her.

She wanted to feel good about the fact that nothing had happened for over twenty-four hours. She wanted to believe that the nightmare was over.

Instead, she had a prickling dread that the danger hadn't gone away at all, that it was out there, building, waiting. So she had come to Miller's class—she had to learn to manage this fear if she was going to have to keep living with it.

Just as she was going to have to learn to manage her feelings for Miller.

She took notes as Miller went down a list of techniques for mental preparation for crime defense. He exuded easy confidence and cool authority, and there wasn't a pindrop of noise in the room as he described the mental approach police used in their training to handle life-threatening situations. Clearly and concisely, he delivered example after example of citizens who'd survived attacks using the principles of reacting and resisting—being *mentally prepared* to react and resist.

Some things surprised her.

"Expect to be hurt," he told the class. "If you're afraid to be hurt, you'll be afraid to resist.

"Don't wait for the perfect chance to escape," he said later. "The perfect chance might never come."

Mind setting, he hammered home between every point, could save your life. "Never give up," he concluded when the class was over. "Never, never, never."

When he'd started talking, his examples of violence and resistance to violence had made Natalie's already edgy nerves ache. But by the time he'd finished, she was surprised to find the pall that had been hanging over her for days had shifted, and with it the fear, shifted, transforming into something that utilized her anger and made her feel strong. Still scared, but ready to deal with anything.

"Hi there."

She looked up from stuffing her pocket-sized spiral notebook into her purse. Miller stood by her desk. The class had emptied fast. From her seated position, he looked impossibly tall.

Impossibly sexy.

She couldn't blame herself for noticing. What woman wouldn't notice?

"Hi," she said back. "Great class."

"I'm glad you came," he said. "How are you doing?"

He wasn't touching her, but she could feel the familiar warmth of his body in her too sensitive pulse points.

"I'm doing fine," she said carefully.

A subtle smile danced in his eyes, finally touching his stern mouth.

"Fine. You always say that, you know."

"Well, it's true." Natalie scooted out of her seat and stood, swinging her purse strap over her shoulder. "Most of the time," she added with a little laugh.

Reluctantly, she pulled her gaze away from his, looked at the door. She should go home.

Miller's voice stopped her. "Do you have a minute? I'd like to talk to you."

"Okay."

"There haven't been any incidents? Any phone calls or anything? I didn't see any reports come in."

She shook her head.

"No," she said. "Nothing. Just . . . silence. Maybe it's over."

"Maybe."

The way he said it made the hair on the back of her neck stand up. She knew he didn't think it was over.

"Do you mind if we take a walk outside? The weather's great today, and you look like you could use some fresh air."

Natalie gave him a sideways look.

"Hey, you look beautiful," he said. "I didn't mean anything rude by that."

He laughed, which had her blushing in embarrassment as he held the door open for her before joining her in the hall. They headed down the corridor toward the back of the community center.

"I just meant that you look tired," he explained as they walked side by side. "You're still not sleeping, are you?"

Natalie shrugged. "Not as much as usual," she admitted.

Miller ducked into a small kitchenette near the back door. He grabbed a deli bag out of the mini-fridge, and then inserted enough coins for two chilled sodas from a drink machine. They were cherry colas. His favorite, she remembered with a pang.

The more time she spent with him, the more the little things came back to her.

Handing one of the cans to Natalie, he said, "I have thirty minutes till the next session. I do the same class in the afternoon. I hope you don't mind talking over lunch."

Natalie thanked him for the drink and tried to turn down his offer of half his submarine sandwich, but Miller insisted.

"You look like you haven't been eating right, either," he said.

He was right, and she was touched by his concern, but the tenuous nature of their current relationship made her uncomfortable. It seemed as if he was handling it all right.

She didn't know how to tell him that she wasn't handling it all right, too. She didn't know how to tell him how much it hurt.

They walked side by side outside, the sunny day almost painful in its contrast to the situation threatening to engulf her. They followed the paved pathway leading out from the rear door of the community center. This was the largest of Silver City's five public parks, containing a duck pond, a playground, and picnic tables.

Since it was a Saturday, and the first day in a week without at least a sprinkling of rain, the park was bustling with families. They picked a bench near the bright, sparkling water.

While she ate, Natalie focused on a family of white ducks swimming in a neat vee across the big pond. Miller filled her in on the investigation's progress in the past twenty-four hours.

There had been no prints found on the box that had arrived in her office. No luck finding where the mouse had been purchased or any information uncovered regarding the dark sedan that had tried to run her down in the parking lot of the hospital.

He'd followed up on all the laid-off workers from Universal Technologies, whether they'd come in for fingerprinting or not.

"Ethan Parrish has a record in Arkansas. He was eighteen years old. Assault and battery. He served ten months for beating up his high school girlfriend on the night of the prom."

Natalie was floored.

"I wonder if Ginny knows about this. Why didn't my father know about it?" She knew Universal Technologies routinely asked for criminal information from prospective employees.

"It must have slipped by," Miller said. "It happens. Employees don't report it on their applications, and personnel offices slip up in their background checks. It's not that unusual for ex-cons to get jobs without ever telling their employers they've been in prison. They just keep applying for jobs until somebody hires them without checking."

Natalie stared at him. "Ginny didn't come in to work on Friday."

"Let me know if you hear anything from her. I tried to get in touch with her on Friday myself, with no luck. She agreed to come in to be fingerprinted, but she never showed up."

Natalie finished most of her half of the sandwich before putting it down, swallowing over the lump in her throat. She didn't know what to think.

Could Ginny or Ethan be involved in what was happening to her?

Or was it a faceless stranger?

"What are they waiting for?" She was holding the cold soda can in her hands, the chill from the liquid seeming to seep into her heart.

She stood, poked the can into a nearby trash bin, and walked the few steps to the edge of the pond. She had a couple of bites of sandwich left, and she tore it in pieces, tossing it to the ducks, who flapped at the water and raced for the floating bread.

She sensed Miller coming up behind her.

"Is this part of the game, making me wait, wonder?" she asked, still staring at the ducks. "Is the idea to make me go completely insane?"

Miller reached out, touched her shoulder. "I don't know."

She squeezed her eyes shut for a precious, strength-gathering second. His words reminded her not to depend on him. He didn't know the answers—no one did. She had to depend on herself. Nothing had been more clear about the personal defense techniques Miller had taught today than the fact that every person had to depend on her own inner mental strength to carry her.

"It's time for me to get going," she said finally, turning to look at him. "And you have your next class coming up."

"Don't let your guard down, Nat. I hope this is over, but chances are, it's not."

Miller wanted to touch Natalie so desperately that he shook with the need. He was an idiot, the biggest idiot on earth.

"I'll walk you to your car," he said.

She nodded, smiled tightly, and he saw regret printed in her eyes—as if she wanted to say something else. Or wanted him to say something else.

But whatever it was, she kept it to herself.

"Ginny, please call me when you get in." Natalie hung up the phone, staring at it in dissatisfaction on Sunday afternoon.

Leaving another message didn't cut it.

Natalie had left several messages over the weekend already, without getting a callback.

She grabbed her purse and keys and headed for the garage. A prickly fear had kept her from going to Ginny's apartment today, but she shook it off.

She had to check on her, make sure she was all right. She considered—then dismissed—the idea of calling Brad, asking him to accompany her.

When Brad had finally called her back last night, he'd confessed to being under the weather. There was no point in disturbing him when he was sick.

It was a five-minute drive to Ginny's apartment complex. The Spanish-style architecture, with its crisp orange-tiled roof and whitewashed walls, exuded a solid, comfortable ambience.

Ginny had a first-floor apartment in the third building. She enjoyed growing plants on the back patio and had a collection of whimsical pewter wind chimes that she loved.

Natalie couldn't hear the chimes now, but the sluggish air was barely moving today.

She rang the bell, then knocked on the door for good measure. Nothing happened.

She went around to the back. The air lifted just slightly, and the familiar tinkle of a wind chime carried on the breeze as she came to the patio. A cheerful medley of flowers and ivies tumbled out of an assortment of ceramic and plastic pots. A hummingbird feeder hung on a hook extended from the patio wall, filled halfway with red liquid.

Everything looked completely normal until she stared into the apartment through the sliding glass patio door, its beige drapes pushed open. Her heart started banging, and her throat closed.

The apartment had been completely trashed.

ELEVEN

The marbled lobby of Silver City National Bank oozed the plush splendor afforded by a century of money, celebrated in the free twenty-five-dollar savings bonds offered for opening a new account in their centennial year. Miller sidestepped the queue of Monday-morning customers at the main counter and approached a receptionist whose desk obstructed access to the carpeted corridor of private offices.

"I'd like to see Mr. Harrison. Brad Harrison," he added to clarify between Brad and his father, Philip Harrison. He knew both men kept offices here in the main branch of the bank. "You can tell him Miller Brannigan is here."

"Oh, yes. You're the one who called last week, right?" the receptionist asked.

Miller nodded. He'd been trying to get in touch with Brad since Friday as part of his overall canvassing of Natalie's friends and coworkers. Events over the weekend had only increased his interest in interviewing Brad, though he recognized that his own personal feelings might have as much to do with his desire to grill the man as any actual facts did.

Natalie had called him early Sunday afternoon from the property manager's office at Ginny's apartment complex. He'd driven straight over to meet her there and examine the wreckage of the apartment.

Most of Ginny's clothes and personal belongings were gone—and so was Ginny. None of the neighbors had seen or heard anything.

All Miller was left with was an unshakable sense of escalating danger—but he had no idea where it was coming from.

He watched the receptionist punch a button on the intercom phone, her dark eyes curious.

"Mr. Harrison, an Officer Brannigan would like to speak with you." She put the phone down seconds later. "Mr. Harrison will see you." She stood and led the way down the corridor.

Brad met them at the door of his office. The receptionist hovered.

"Thank you, Stephanie," Brad dismissed her. He shut the office door.

Miller waited for Brad to walk back around his massive desk. The surface was a gleaming dark wood. There were papers stacked in piles as neat as the expensive suit Brad wore.

"Have a seat, Miller. I don't have much time. I assume this is about Natalie, not a social call."

Beneath his expertly cut sandy hair, Brad's face was an impassive mask, yet Miller sensed a coiled intensity radiating from the man. The tension was hard to read. Miller knew too well that it could be mixed with a subtle—and not so subtle—rivalry that went back years, all the way to high school.

They'd never been enemies—or friends. But they'd both been close to Natalie.

Brad was still close to Natalie.

"This is just routine," Miller said, sitting across from Brad. "I'm checking with Natalie's friends, acquaintances, anyone who might have information about who could be perpetrating this string of incidents."

"And you think I might have information."

"Do you?"

Brad's smooth expression broke, revealing a crease of clear concern. He sighed and shook his head. "Wish I did," he said.

"You can't think of anyone who might have a motive for giving Natalie grief?"

Impatience flickered across Brad's face.

"Natalie's pretty low-key," he said. "She doesn't have enemies."

"You were out of town this weekend," Miller probed. Frustrated and restless after leaving Natalie on Sunday afternoon, he'd swung by Brad's condominium complex. Brad hadn't been there, but Miller had lucked into a chatty neighbor outside the condo next door.

Mrs. Blakeley was a retired minister's wife. She was decidedly disapproving of Brad Harrison, and didn't mind talking about him. At length.

Brad took his time before answering.

"That's right," he said finally. "I was out of town. A business trip. I didn't find out about the incident Thursday night at Natalie's town house until yesterday, when I spoke with her on the phone. I wish I'd known, so I could have been the one to be there for her. She needs her friends now."

The way his eyes sharpened revealed that he knew Miller was the one who'd been there for Natalie that night, and Brad didn't like it.

Miller had to admit to himself that he wouldn't like it if the opposite were the case, if Brad had been the one to be there for Natalie that night. It was idiotic. Both of them had the same goal: Natalie's well-being.

Miller had no right to be possessive of her. Did Brad have a right?

He wouldn't think so, considering Mrs. Blakeley's comments regarding Brad's ongoing affair with a regular overnight female guest.

Still, there was this subtle possessiveness, even in Brad's tone when he spoke Natalie's name, and it irritated the hell out of Miller.

"How well do you know Ginny Moore?" Miller asked, shifting gears.

Brad gave a nearly imperceptible shrug.

"Not well," he responded. "She's a friend of Natalie's, so we're acquainted. Natalie's very worried about Ginny. So am I."

"Can you think of any reason Ginny might want to hurt Natalie?"

Brad frowned. "Of course not. But that would

be convenient for you, wouldn't it? The incidents stop, and Ginny disappears. You can't solve the case, so you cover your ass by blaming Ginny."

"No one's blaming Ginny for anything," Miller said in a level voice.

"Well, what are you doing to find Ginny, then?" the other man challenged. "Her disappearance doesn't make sense. She leaves her home, her job, her friends, without a word. Her apartment is destroyed. It's obvious something's not right, and equally obvious what it is."

Brad stood, walking around his desk as he went on: "What if the nutcase who was after Natalie has moved on to Ginny?"

Miller stood, met Brad at the door to his office.

"We haven't ruled anything out," he said. A muscle in his jaw tightened.

Brad rubbed him the wrong way, but that was no reason to dismiss his comments, even if Brad's scenario seemed unlikely. The truth was, in this case, nothing made sense. Was Ginny's disappearance connected to Natalie's case? Or was it possibly a domestic violence incident between Ginny and Ethan?

Based on Parrish's history, Miller's suspicions leaned toward the latter.

He wanted to question Ethan Parrish, but so far he hadn't been able to find the former Universal Technologies worker. It was starting to look as if Parrish was missing, too.

Pausing in the office doorway, Miller turned

back to Brad. They were the same height and faced each other eye to eye.

"You fly your own plane," Miller commented casually.

"That's right. I've been flying since I was fourteen. Anything else you want to know, Brannigan?"

"You take a lot of *business* trips to Las Vegas?" Miller inquired.

Miller had followed up on something else the retired minister's wife had dropped, and had visited the small, private airstrip outside town. The information he'd gotten from the airstrip's manager had been interesting—if not necessarily significant.

Brad narrowed his eyes. "You'll have to excuse me," he said in a low, taut voice. "I have a meeting in two minutes."

Miller nodded. "Have a good day."

He strode past Brad, emerging a few moments later into the surprisingly hot April morning. He crossed the parking lot to his police cruiser, wondering what, if anything, he'd accomplished.

The temp receptionist buzzed a call through at four-thirty Monday afternoon. Natalie picked up, her attention still fixed on the financial analysis on her computer screen.

"Brad! Hi."

"How are you?"

"Hey, I'm not the one who's been sick. How

are *you?"* She swiveled her chair, facing away from her computer. Outside, the sun beat down on the stone buildings of the town square. Light glinted off the courthouse's elaborate metal roof.

Birds swooped in the bright afternoon, landing in the blossoming cherry trees on the courthouse lawn. She felt a surge of spring fever that took her by surprise, reminded her what normal life felt like.

She wished her normal life was back, but with Ginny missing, she felt more uneasy than ever. The sense of danger lying in wait hadn't gone away.

When would she feel safe to walk outside in the sunshine without worrying that someone was watching her from the shadows?

"I'm feeling fine," Brad said.

"Great." She turned away from the window, waiting for Brad to tell her why he was calling.

There was a strange silence on the line.

"Brad?"

"I have to tell you something, Nat."

She didn't like the sound of Brad's voice. Something was wrong.

"What?"

"I wasn't completely honest with you."

She swallowed, clenched the phone tighter. "What do you mean?" Instinctively, she knew what was coming even before he said it and was angry at herself, at everything that was happening that had kept her from seeing it, from knowing Brad was in trouble again.

"I wasn't sick this weekend. I was gambling."

Natalie squeezed her eyes shut.

"Brad," she breathed, disappointment cutting so deep that it hurt.

"Brannigan knows, and I didn't want you to hear it from him."

"Miller knows?" Confusion whirled together with her frustration.

"He was in my office today, asking questions. About Ginny, mostly. But he found out somehow—He knew that I'd been making trips to Vegas. I'm sorry, Nat."

"Brad. You promised that was over, that you weren't going to—"

"I know. I can't explain it or excuse it. It's a relief, really, to tell someone."

Natalie sighed, fatigue pressing on her suddenly. She couldn't remember the last time she'd had a full night's sleep.

"Brad, you have to get help." She pressed her fingertips against her aching forehead.

"I know. You're right. I can get through this. I know I can. I'm going to get back into counseling. Everything's going to work out."

He sounded desolate despite his words. She knew how hard he'd worked to get through his addiction once, and now he had to do it a second time. She was angry and heartbroken for him at the same time.

"I don't want you to worry about this right now, Nat," he went on, his voice gentle, low. She had to strain to hear him, press the phone tighter to her ear. "You have enough to worry about. We're going to take care of you first."

"Brad . . ." Emotion choked her throat.

There was another long silence on the line.

"Remember what we used to say?" he asked. "Remember how when we were kids we used to say that if we were thirty and not married, we'd marry each other?"

"We're not thirty." She remembered how positively ancient they'd thought thirty was in those days.

"Close enough."

The marriage proposal was a running joke, so she recognized his attempt at lightening the mood. "One of these days I'm going to say yes and you're going to absolutely die, because you're going to have to figure out how to let me down easy."

The receptionist poked her head in, waving a pink phone message. Natalie nodded, and the receptionist brought her the note.

"Brad, I'm sorry. I have to go. We'll talk later, okay?"

She hung up, staring at the phone message. *Ginny Moore, line two.* She punched the button to pick up the other line.

"Ginny?"

The line was dead.

Natalie woke harshly, sweat beading between her breasts. The phone's ring sounded shrill in the darkness. She reached first for the switch on the lamp by her bed, squinting in reaction to the light.

She grabbed the phone. The clock on her nightstand read eleven-forty.

It had been after eleven the last time she'd checked her clock. She'd slept for a whopping half hour at the most.

"Hello?"

Silence. A chill shook her, chasing away the nervous sweat.

"Hello?" she whispered again, her voice thready, unreal. Across the room, the closet doors were shut and a feeling scarcely recalled from childhood washed over her. She remembered how scared she used to be of monsters—in the closet, under the bed, behind doors.

Now, the monsters were everywhere—and nowhere.

At her feet, she felt movement. She nearly screamed before she realized it was Prissy.

"Natalie."

The voice was so soft, the thundering of her heart nearly drowned it out.

"Ginny?"

"It's me," Ginny whispered. "I'm sorry to wake you up. I'm sorry about everything." Her voice hitched into a sob.

"Are you all right? Where are you? What's going on?" Natalie volleyed questions.

"Tell me you're okay. I'm worried about you."

"Ginny! I'm fine. I'm worried about *you!*"

"I have to see you. Will you meet me?"

"Meet you where?"

Ginny named an all-night grocery store.

"I'm calling from the phone booth out front, by the newspaper machine," she said. "I'll watch for you. Please come."

"Just come here," Natalie suggested, confused by the strange request.

"I can't. I—Natalie, please come. I know it's late, but I don't have much time."

"Why? Ginny, what's going on?"

Ginny was talking, but it came out muffled, as if she'd moved the phone away from her mouth to do something else—or talk to someone else. Natalie made out Ethan's name, but she wasn't sure.

"What? What about Ethan?" she asked. "Ginny?" She heard a click, and the connection was gone.

Natalie tore out of bed, pulled on jeans and a sweatshirt. She felt the delicate metal of the heart and chain necklace slide against her neck and flop over the sweatshirt. She pushed it back inside her clothes, next to her skin.

It was the heart necklace Miller had given her years ago. She'd taken to wearing it under her clothes the last few days, hidden where she wouldn't have to explain to anyone why she was wearing it.

Downstairs, she checked the caller identification box. It said "pay phone" and listed the number. She considered calling back but decided against it. She didn't know what was going on, but she needed to get to Ginny as fast as possible.

The one thing she was certain about was that Ginny was scared, and calling back might spook her.

Grabbing her purse, Natalie looked at the phone again. Was it safe to meet Ginny alone?

Her mind flung instantly to Miller. Should she call him, wake him up, ask him to meet her?

This was crazy, she thought angrily. Ginny was one of her closest friends, and she actually thought Ginny might hurt her, or be connected to someone who might hurt her.

She was sick of the fear, sick of the doubt.

She was tired of being scared. She was reclaiming her life, starting now. She wasn't going to wait for someone to come hold her hand before she went to Ginny. That was ridiculous.

Prissy followed her to the garage door, whimpering at her feet, jumping at her ankles.

"Oh, all right." She scooped the little dog into her arms and took her to the car. Prissy was as anxious as she was at the activity at this hour, and the truth was, Natalie could use some company.

She backed the car out, closed the garage door. The car's engine hummed softly. The streets were empty. She turned out of her cul-de-sac and onto the main thoroughfare, heading for Chief Foods.

Silver City was hushed at this hour, at least in this sedate part of town. Streetlights spilled eery sweeps of light over the neat, manicured avenue. At regularly spaced intervals, beds of colorful spring blossoms brightened the grassy center median, garish in the unnatural light.

Pushing her foot to the floor at a yellow light, she pressed ahead. She slowed only when she reached the grocery store's enormous parking lot. There weren't more than a dozen cars, parked up close to the building. She could see a man coming through one of the automatic doors, a paper shopping sack in his arms.

Light blazed out of the huge plate-glass windows across the front of the building. There was a pay phone next to the newspaper machine.

It was the phone Ginny had identified as the one she was calling from.

Natalie swallowed, glancing around. Where was Ginny? She pulled up in the space directly in front of the pay phone and checked the doors. She was safe, in front of the store, locked in.

She waited.

Twenty minutes had passed when she heard the sirens. She thought they were police sirens, but when she craned her head around to look, she saw a fire engine rushing by, followed by a second one.

She sighed. The sirens had made her think of Miller. She was glad she hadn't called him, woken him up for nothing. She would have felt foolish.

In the morning she could call him and tell him about it. Not because the information was terribly valuable. She wasn't sure what Miller could possibly do with it. But she would use the excuse to hear his voice. Stupid, but there it was.

Thinking about Miller had the predictable result of making her heart ache, and the adrenaline rush of frustration and anger that had carried her out of the town house and to the grocery store seeped away. Fatigue followed in its wake.

How could she reclaim her life until she knew what was going on? She had no idea whether Ginny's strange behavior was connected to her own situation. She had no idea if she'd ever be victimized again.

Maybe the person who'd been harassing her had bored of their game, gone away. She might never know why it had happened in the first place, and would never be sure exactly when it was okay to stop being afraid.

Prissy burrowed into Natalie's sweatshirt, her little body shivering. After an unusually warm day, the temperature had dropped considerably at nightfall.

Natalie looked at the clock on her dashboard. Another ten minutes. It had been half an hour now, and still no Ginny.

She moved Prissy back to the passenger seat and keyed the ignition. She turned on the heater and circled the parking lot. There was another pay phone at the far end, but no signs of life were to be found there, either. She was worried, but what could she do? There was nothing to do but go home and hope Ginny was all right, that she would contact her again.

She drove back down the familiar, broad street, lined with nice, comfortable homes where families slept peacefully in their beds. Silver City was so normal, so incredibly, impossibly normal.

But underneath, was the small town really peaceful? She'd found out in the past week that her two closest friends had secrets.

Earlier in the evening, she'd spent over an hour on the phone with Brad, encouraging him again to get back into therapy. She understood him and was always willing to listen, but she knew that the root of his problems required professional help. Being a Harrison of the Silver City Harrisons was no easy task.

No matter how hard Brad worked to fill the role of leading citizen of the town, as his family expected, there was a side of him that hated his expected position, tried to destroy it. He had to get help—before he destroyed himself.

But at least she knew, understood, what was happening to Brad. Ginny's plight was a mystery.

The boulevard curled around west, and between the tall trees and rooftops she caught glimpses of an ominous flaring light. She remembered the fire engines, and realized that the blaze to which they'd been responding was in her neighborhood.

Her neighborhood.

Nausea swelled in her throat. She gripped the steering wheel tightly as she swung onto the residential street off the boulevard, heading toward her street. There were people out in their pajamas or with clothes that looked hastily flung on, running toward her cul-de-sac.

It was blocked by fire engines, and Natalie parked haphazardly at the corner, leaving Prissy in the vehicle yapping in protest at being left behind.

Natalie ran toward the building that was on fire. *Her building.* There was no sensation of surprise, just a surreal numbness.

Flames licked the dark sky, transforming it into an unnatural dawn. Torrents of water rained down from hoses connected to fire trucks.

She kept running until one of the firemen stepped in her path, grabbed hold of her arm.

"Lady, you can't go any closer!"

"That's my house," she cried.

Even as she stood there, the roof caved in on the connected row of town houses, a sheet of flames shooting up as it went down.

"It's gone, ma'am. It's gone. There's nothing you can do. Be grateful you weren't in there."

Be grateful you weren't in there. She thought of Ginny's strange call. *If Ginny hadn't called and insisted on meeting her, she might be dead.*

The knowledge rocked her, but she was hopeless to know what it meant. Her mind was functioning in a dreamlike state.

"Did everyone get out?" She looked around dizzily, worrying about her neighbors. There were huddles of people, some from her building, some she didn't recognize.

"Are you Natalie Buchanan?" the fireman yelled over the cacophony of crackling flames and spewing water and voices.

She nodded.

"Then everyone's out," he shouted. "Your neighbors thought you were still in there. We tried to go in to find you, but it was too late. The building was already completely involved. It went up fast."

"What happened?" All she could do was stare in horror. Somewhere a window shattered in the heat. Embers flew in the air.

Her home was gone; everything was gone.

Thank God she'd brought Prissy with her.

The fireman shook his head. "We won't know until there's been an investigation, ma'am. But one of your neighbors was awake, called the police about a prowler just before the fire started. We'll need a statement from you. Don't go anywhere."

He turned, noticing a group of onlookers approaching. "Get back," he ordered, striding toward them.

Natalie's legs trembled. She drew in a sharp breath, coughed on the smoky air, and watched her world crumpling into a heap of firewood.

The nightmare was back with a vengeance. She knew it, without a doubt. This was directed at her.

Someone had set fire to her town house, putting at risk everyone else in the building. They all could have died—because of her. *Because someone was after her—and they weren't going to stop.*

What did they want?

Did they want her dead?

What would happen when they found out they'd failed tonight, that she was still alive?

Staggering backward in rising panic, all she could think about was running. She didn't know where she could go, and it didn't matter. She just had to get away from here. As far away as possible.

Her heart slammed crazily and she whirled, thudding directly into a hard body. The collision knocked the breath out of her.

"Natalie!" Miller grabbed her shoulders. "I thought you were—" He broke off, his face streaked with sweat, his eyes hot with a wild relief. He smelled like smoke and desperation, and he was looking at her as if she were the most precious thing in the world. "I thought—Oh, God, Natalie," he rasped, emotion shaking his voice. Then he was cupping her face, kissing her everywhere—her forehead, her eyelids, her nose.

And for that moment she let herself cling to him, to life, to everything that had ever really mattered.

TWELVE

Miller filled his arms with Natalie's warmth and softness as the deepest despair he'd ever known turned to joy. *She was all right.* The relief was almost dizzying, and if he hadn't been holding *her* up, he might have lost his own balance.

For horrible, God-awful minutes, he'd thought she was dead. But she wasn't. She was in his arms, and if he was dreaming, he didn't want to wake up.

He tangled his fingers in her hair, buried his face in the sweet scent of her. "I was at home," he whispered roughly, holding her tighter. "I couldn't sleep. I have a police scanner, and the call came in about a prowler."

He pulled back then, needing to see her as well as touch her. He couldn't get enough of her.

"By the time I made it across town," he went on, "the fire trucks were already here. I thought you were in there. I thought it was too late. You scared me to death."

The hellishly shimmering rubble of her home spit and crackled behind them. Heat emanated in scorching waves from the burning building, but in his embrace Natalie shivered. He rubbed her arms.

"Are you all right?" He held his breath, scrutinizing her face. "Are you hurt?"

She shook her head.

"I wasn't home. Ginny called. She wanted me to meet her, but when I got there, she was gone. If she hadn't called—" She stopped abruptly, squeezed her eyes shut for a second, then lifted them to him, wide and hurt. "If she hadn't called, I might be dead. Do you think—oh, God—do you think she knew?"

The pain and confusion in her voice hit him hard. He pushed back the strands of hair that fell in her face, tucking them behind one ear. Rage uncoiled inside him.

"I don't know," he said quietly, forcing his voice to be gentle when inside he wanted to smash something. *Someone.* Whoever had set this fire tonight. "I'm just thanking God you weren't home."

"They're not going to stop till they kill me," she whispered.

A sickening coil of anger burned in his gut, fueled by his fear for Natalie.

"That's not going to happen."

"I thought it was over," she said. "But it's not over. They burned my house down. My neighbors—They could have killed people! Not just me, but total strangers! As it is, my neighbors have lost everything. They could have died. It would have been my fault!"

"It wouldn't have been your fault. None of this is your fault."

"They're after *me!*" she cried, anger infusing her voice now.

She was trembling, and he didn't know if it was the terror or the exhaustion, or the chilly wind that whipped through the scorching heat waving out from the fire. A cold front was moving in.

Rain was predicted before morning—ironic now, in the face of Natalie's burning home.

In the flickering light, Natalie's skin looked nearly translucent, and he realized that she'd lost weight just in the past week. She was too thin, and her eyes were drained of hope.

He was determined to change that.

"They're not going to get you," he said, gently shaking her. "I'm not going to let them. *You're* not going to let them."

Her eyes were wild with anguish.

"I'm losing it," she breathed roughly. "I'm sorry."

She tried to whirl away from him, but he wasn't letting her go. He yanked her back into his arms.

"You're not losing it. You're fine. You're always *fine,* remember?"

She let out a half-laugh, half-sob.

"You're alive," he repeated fiercely. "That's all that matters." He struggled to moderate his voice. He was furious, but not with her. "And you're going to stay that way."

Activity carried on as firefighters shouted to each other and rushed back and forth. The crowd surrounding the scene kept growing. Nobody seemed to notice two people standing in the soaked grass in the middle of all the confusion.

"I have to get away from here," Natalie whispered, her gaze darting desperately.

He knew what she was afraid of—that they *weren't* unnoticed. That someone was out there, watching.

Someone who wished her harm. "You're in no shape to drive."

"I'm fine," she protested immediately. "You just said so."

"When's the last night you slept more than two hours straight?"

Her legs looked as if they were going to give out from under her any second. He didn't bide his time for her to answer, just bent slightly, swung her into his arms, and started marching.

He wasn't waiting for her to admit that she needed anything, much less help. The need to protect her, whether she wanted his protection or not, was too strong.

He'd realized something when he'd pulled up to her town house, seen it going up in smoke— and believed she was inside. What he felt in his heart for Natalie was real. It was deep, and it was abiding. It wasn't mere physical attraction, and it wasn't something that would go away if he just ignored it long enough.

When he'd seen the fire and had thought he'd

lost her, he'd known the enormous consequences of not dealing with his extraordinary feelings—and not finding out if she felt the same way.

He'd been too afraid of being a fool again. So he'd been a coward.

But not now. He had another chance, and he was grabbing it with both hands.

"You're in no shape to drive."

"What are you doing?" She pushed at his chest, but he wouldn't let go. "I told you I was fine."

He'd expected a fight.

"Good. Glad to hear it." He kept moving, striding through the chaos to his car. Thank God he wasn't blocked in.

Her arms clamped around his neck for balance if nothing else.

"You don't have to carry me."

He never broke stride.

"I can walk!"

"Of course you can," he said smoothly. When they got to the car, he set her on her feet and opened the passenger side door. "But now you don't have to."

She bristled with annoyance, but the way she immediately reached out to the car door for support told him the truth. She'd been running on empty for too many days and was a lot more wobbly than she cared to admit.

A dandelion puff was probably sturdier than she was at that moment.

"They said they needed a statement," she said.

"We can take care of that tomorrow—after you've slept ten or twenty hours."

She sat down in the car and he shut the door.

"Prissy!" she gasped when he'd settled himself in the driver's seat. "My car's over there." She pointed.

He stopped the car at the corner and she retrieved the dog from her front seat, then locked her car. She sat down with the dog yapping hoarsely on her lap, as if it had been yapping for a long time.

They drove down the boulevard that cut through town. Light from streetlamps slashed across the car, broken by shadows. He glanced at Natalie. The fight had gone out of her fast. She stared out the window.

"I guess I should be asking where we're going," she said tonelessly, turning her face to him. "I can't go to a friend's house, or my father's. I can't go any place that whoever is doing this might track me to. I can't jeopardize my friends, my father."

A streetlight lanced over them as he took a left, heading for the on ramp to Highway 54.

Natalie's stomach rolled as the next thought washed over her.

"I can't jeopardize *you*," she said suddenly. The idea of something happening to Miller, and it being her fault, made her feel sick.

She was confused about practically everything, but not about this—she couldn't be responsible for hurting Miller. She'd hurt him enough in the past, hadn't she?

"I'm a cop," he said. He quirked a brow. "I live for danger."

"Very funny," she said. "But I'm serious. I don't want anything to happen to you. You have to get rid of me, now. Take me to a hotel. Take me to the Huffington. They have security."

The Huffington had been built by a relative newcomer to Silver City's business community. The family-owned luxury hotel had been established in partnership with theaters, restaurants, and a new museum, linking a modern entertainment district with the historic center of town. The Huffington family had provided a private security force to patrol the area in order to attract tourism with a promise of protection.

It was the safest place in Silver City. If such a thing as safety existed for her. Natalie wasn't so sure of that anymore.

"That's exactly where anyone who knows you would expect you to go," Miller said.

Natalie chewed her lip. She threw up her hands.

"Fine, then I suppose you'd recommend the Red Sage Motor Lodge."

The Red Sage charged by the hour. She read about it every week in the paper. There were regular drug busts in the parking lot.

Miller laughed. "I don't think so. You'd better stick with me, sweetheart."

"I don't want to put you in danger," she insisted softly.

He reached over, covered her hand with his. In

the darkness, his eyes gleamed with more emotion than she was equipped to handle.

More emotion than she trusted herself to be perceiving correctly.

Sure, Miller had been glad to discover that she hadn't died in the fire. Sure, he'd kissed her and held her, and she'd almost forgotten for a miraculous second how much trouble she was in.

But he wasn't interested in picking up where they'd left off so long ago. He'd made that clear, and she wasn't stupid enough to hope he'd changed his mind.

Which did nothing to explain why that look in his eyes made her want to cry.

"I can protect myself, Nat," he said with quiet strength. He squeezed her hand. "I'm not leaving you, so give it up. I'm not going to 'get rid' of you—and there's no way you can get rid of me. We're going to get through this—and we're going to do it together."

Outside, it started sprinkling. Pats of rain struck the top of the car and the windshield, cocooning them, and the world that had turned so nightmarish all of a sudden seemed far away, unreal.

"Thank you," she whispered, realizing without a doubt that just as surely as Miller had stolen her heart ten years ago, he'd stolen it again tonight.

THIRTEEN

They stayed on Highway 54 for six miles, then turned onto a farm-to-market road that cut deep into the rough countryside. Drizzle turned to deluge, and in the car's headlights, Natalie could see nothing but wet blacktop unwinding ahead of them, fence posts whizzing by on either side. Darkness shrouded the surrounding rugged, hilly ranchland that she knew was there.

Natalie gripped the dash as the vehicle veered off onto an unmarked gravel lane. She almost missed the mailbox, scarcely making out the name. Farrell.

"Are we almost there?" she asked. Miller had said he had a quiet place outside town where they could stay. She'd figured he meant he had an apartment in one of the new developments that had been springing up like weeds around the town's boundaries in the past few years—single-family homes and multifamily dwellings alike.

But they'd passed the last of them a mile back, before they'd turned off on the farm-to-market route.

Miller braked almost immediately after taking the gravel lane, the tires slipping a bit in the water-logged road base before the car came to an abrupt stop. In the headlights Natalie could see a metal gate. A closed metal gate.

"Hang on." He took off his seat belt, turned off the car, and grabbed his keys out of the ignition. "Be right back."

He got out, the storm rushing in with vigor no matter how fast he tried to shut the door behind him. Rain sprayed in on the hard wind, splattering the driver's seat and hitting Natalie across the lap. It was a cold rain, and she shivered as she watched Miller hurriedly unlocking and swinging open the massive metal contraption that barred the entrance.

When he and the storm slammed back in, he was drenched to the skin. Rivulets of rain streamed down his face. But in the darkness, his eyes gleamed, and she knew that wherever they were, it was a place that made Miller happy.

"We're here," he said.

"Where's here?" Natalie asked as the car moved forward again over the rutted gravel, but even as she asked, their destination appeared through the driving rain, lit up by the car's beams.

The gravel lane dead-ended in front of a large, two-story house. Pale yellow siding with maroon trim presented a cheerful facade, yet there was something mournful-looking about it, with its dark, vacant windows. As if the only things alive in this desolate place were the elements—the rain and the wind.

The name on the mailbox clicked suddenly in her mind. Miller stopped the car on the drive in front of the steps leading up to the wide porch.

She looked at him. "This is the Farrells' home," she said. "John and Emily."

He nodded. "They left it to me in their will," he explained briefly. He gestured toward the porch. "Come on. Hurry."

Natalie reached under the seat, grabbed Prissy, and made a run for the house. Miller was already soaked, and she was, too, by the time they hit the steps. Prissy quivered in her arms as they sheltered under the porch's meager protection.

Rain drove in sideways on the wind. Miller jabbed a key in the lock, pushed the door open, and held it wide for Natalie to go in ahead of him.

She stepped into the darkness, the air cold and a little thick, and she sensed again the home's disuse. Her feeling was underscored when he hit the lights. She found herself in a small entry hall with a staircase straight ahead and rooms shooting off to either side.

Behind her, Miller slammed the door shut. Wiping her wet shoes on the carpeted mat in the entry, Natalie stepped to her left, drawn by the spacious living area. The entry hall light blazed into the room, revealing bulky leather furniture and a taste for Western art and decor. There was a small bronze of a horse and rider on the coffee table, an Indian blanket draped over the couch, cowboy paintings on the wall, and Texas art and history books lining the built-in shelves.

Everything looked carefully selected, and loved. Natalie guessed the place had been preserved as is from the time the Farrells had lived there, but there was a thick layer of dust on everything that explained the heavy feeling in the air.

"This place is beautiful," she said honestly. Darkness cloaked the view from huge windows, but she was certain it was going to be incredible when morning came.

She noticed an array of framed photographs placed on the mantel over the fireplace. Crossing the rough-planked wooden floor, she stared up at them. She recognized John Farrell's face from the newspaper reports a year earlier, and she knew the middle-aged woman with kind eyes that he had his arm slung around in various pictures had to be Emily.

It was the photos of the young man who drew her, made her heart thunder wildly, her throat close up. Miller. The Miller she'd known ten years ago—impossibly young.

Sometimes it was too easy to forget how truly young they'd been.

She hadn't known this Miller, the boy who glowed with happiness from these photos. As passionate as the boy she'd known had been, he'd also been intense, edgy. Never this happy. He was shown in various poses, working on the ranch. Another photo showed him graduating from the police academy, flanked by a beaming John and Emily.

She saw his life after she'd left him, and it was good. She wished she'd known this Miller.

But it was her own fault she hadn't. *Get a grip*, she reminded herself.

She was *not* going to get maudlin. If she did, things could get really black, really fast, considering the state of her life at the moment.

She looked up, saw Miller watching her.

"I want you out of those wet clothes," he said demandingly.

A hot shiver worked up her spine.

"Oh, yeah?" She arched a brow teasingly. She knew he didn't mean his words as a come-on, but she was feeling a little punch-drunk tonight, and her inhibition quotient was way down.

He looked embarrassed. Miller Brannigan, cool cop, actually looked *embarrassed*.

"I don't want you getting sick," he said, his voice edged with a husky, fascinating mix of uncertainty and desire.

She was playing a dangerous game, and she wasn't punch-drunk *enough* to continue. Playing a teasing game with Miller was high-risk.

"Where should I change?" she asked, and then reality hit her hard in the stomach. "I, uh, don't have a change of clothes," she pointed out inanely. She didn't have *anything* now.

"Come on," he said, ushering her back out to the entry hall. "Bedrooms are upstairs." He waited at the foot of the stairs till she took the steps ahead of him before continuing. "I gave John and Emily's personal effects—their clothes—to charity before I closed up the house. But I come out here every once in a while, to spend a quiet weekend, so I've got some things here."

She hesitated at the top of the stairs. Miller gestured to the right.

"That way," he said. He reached around her to flip the switch when they came to the open doorway, then walked to the dresser and pulled open a deep bottom drawer.

He pulled out a pair of old jeans and a soft, gray, worn-looking police academy sweatshirt.

"I'll change downstairs," he told her. "You can see if anything in there will do, at least for tonight. Or if you'd like, you can take a shower in the bathroom. I think there's a clean bathrobe in the cabinet there. You can bring your clothes back down and we'll get some laundry going."

Natalie nodded. "Thanks."

Miller left. Natalie put Prissy on the bed and investigated the drawers. Prissy, seeming absolutely exhausted from all the excitement, curled into a ball on the pillow and went straight to sleep.

There was a telephone by the bed, and Natalie thought about calling her father. He would hear about the fire on the news in the morning and be concerned about her, but she didn't want to wake him at this point. There was nothing he could do for her in the middle of the night but worry. She would call him in the morning, first thing.

She turned her attention to the bureau. The drawers were stuffed full of old clothes that she had to resist pulling to her face in order to breathe in Miller's scent. She figured that would definitely be on the maudlin no-no list for tonight.

She found a couple of items that looked as if they might do. In the connecting bathroom, she stripped off her soaked things, letting them fall into a wet bundle on the tile floor. The hard, hot spray of the shower felt wonderful, and she could have stood there forever except she was too tired. When she got out, she tried on the sweatshirt she'd brought from Miller's bureau—but it swallowed her up, and his jeans literally fell off her hips.

Finally, she gave up and searched the cabinet in the bathroom for the robe he'd mentioned. It was dark blue terry, and it felt like heaven when she put it on—soft, thick, and warm. She tied it around her waist, took up her bundle of clothes, and set off to find the laundry room.

When Miller arrived back in the living room, his arms full of an extra load of firewood from the dry stack in the shed, he found Natalie on the throw rug in front of the blazing fire he'd gotten going after he'd changed clothes. She was wrapped in the Indian blanket.

Her eyes were closed and she lay on her side with one arm tucked under her cheek, her damp hair gleaming in the firelight.

He set the wood quietly on the hearth and went to her. Seated on the rug beside her, he fought the urge to touch her. She looked ethereal, delicate and wispily beautiful, like some lost fairy that might disappear.

She opened her eyes slowly, blinked up at him.

"Hey." He smiled down at her. "I didn't mean to wake you."

The confusion in her eyes melted into clarity, and the exact second she remembered everything that had happened was obvious.

"God, it wasn't just a bad dream, was it?" she asked softly.

The pain in her eyes grabbed Miller by the throat. "No," he said. "It was real."

"I was looking for the laundry room," she said, her gaze disconnecting from his, hitting the pile of clothes on the floor by the couch. "I couldn't find it, and I couldn't find you, so I just . . . waited."

She moved to sit up. The blanket slid down, twisted, and fell away, revealing the robe and the long lengths of bare leg below the midthigh hem. Miller's muscles tensed against the onslaught of need for this woman. He wanted to touch her, hold her, protect her—with his life, if necessary.

She was *that* important to him.

He felt linked to her as he'd never felt linked to another human being in his life. But he didn't

want to walk blindly into another relationship
with Natalie Buchanan, despite his gut feeling
that there had been more to what had happened
ten years ago than what he'd seen on the surface
at the time. He still didn't know what that *more*
was, and what it would mean.

Until he did, he would have to be careful.

He watched Natalie pull at the blanket protec-
tively, hugging it around her body. She stared into
the fire, closed in, shielding herself with her arms
and the blanket, her knees drawn up to her
chest—looking stunningly defenseless, anyway.

"I'm the biggest pain in the neck," she said.
"I'm really sorry. I'm sure this isn't what you were
planning to do tonight."

"Plans are made for changing."

She looked at him, and there was something
torturous in her eyes.

"You don't have to feel obligated to me just
because we knew each other in the past," she said.

Miller wished so much to breach her barriers,
to find out—once and for all—what lay behind
the secret shadows in her eyes. But he didn't
know how.

"I don't feel obligated," he argued gently.

She stared down at her knees. "Well, thanks.
But tomorrow I'll figure out somewhere else to
go just the same."

"We'll talk about tomorrow when it comes," he
said. "Don't worry about it tonight. Don't worry
about anything. You're safe here."

He touched her, skimming his fingertips along

her cheek. She hesitated, then slowly, agonizingly, she closed her eyes, leaning into the palm of his hand. Miller didn't move, didn't breathe, just savored the tiny bit of vulnerability she'd let herself reveal.

When she finally straightened, he dared to believe he recognized what he saw in the gaze she lifted up to him. She felt this, too—this desperate, aching bond.

Then, immediately, he could see her drawing back into herself, crossing her arms tighter, pulling the blanket closer. She stared into the fire, unruly locks fanning across her cheek, hiding her.

He reached up and pushed the hair back, tucking it gently behind her ear. In the firelight, a line of gold shimmered through the strands of hair on her neck. The rest of the necklace was hidden. Something teased at the edges of his memory, and without thinking he slipped a finger beneath the chain and lifted it out of the collar of the terry robe.

He slid his fingertips down its delicate links till he grasped the small heart with its diamond sliver.

Recognition startled him. He hadn't seen this necklace in ten years, but he knew it. It was the only gift he'd ever given Natalie.

It had represented their secret pledge to one another. He couldn't afford a ring, and even if he could, Natalie couldn't be engaged to him openly. Not when she was still in high school and her father disapproved of Miller so harshly. So one night, parked in his old car in the shadows of a tree-lined path through Mackenzie Street Park, he'd asked her to marry him, and had given her this gold and diamond heart necklace to hide under her clothes as a reminder of their love and their commitment to each other.

He raised his gaze to search hers as she turned her face toward him. "I remember when I gave you this," he said. "It meant something."

"Yes," she whispered hoarsely. "It did. I want you to know that it did. I want you to know—" She broke off, turned from him—but not before he saw something dark and just beyond his ken pass through her eyes.

Suddenly, he had to know what it was, what hid behind her secret eyes. And he had to know *now.*

"What do you want me to know?" He grabbed her shoulders and shook her gently, until she looked at him. "Tell me," he demanded.

FOURTEEN

She couldn't answer his question with anything but the truth.

"I loved you," Natalie confessed, her heart constricting painfully. "I want you to know that I loved you." The words came out uncensored, honest, barely registering in her brain before they left her lips.

She had no choice. It was far too late for lies. It was probably far too late for the truth, too, but he deserved at least to know it—no matter how much it hurt to tell him.

"If I had it to do over—" Emotion rose so swiftly, it took her breath away.

"If you had it to do over, what?" He dropped his hands from her shoulders but still held her with his penetrating gaze.

She swallowed thickly, then went on, now, while she still had the courage. "If I had it to do over, I wouldn't lie. There was no tour of the fashion houses of Europe. There was no trip to Europe at all. I lied about everything."

Miller's face didn't change, but she saw the

emotion that moved into his eyes. She saw the pain, and knew she had caused it.

"Why?"

She paused, then forced the truth out. "Because I was terrified."

"Of me?" He sounded shocked.

She stared at him, at the tense lines in his face. "Of how much I loved you. And of how much you loved me back."

"I don't understand."

"I don't know if I can make you understand," she whispered, feeling very inadequate to the task and very much terrified all over again. Would he hate her when he knew the truth? It would break her heart if he did, even though she knew deep down that that made no sense. Their chance for a future had been destroyed long ago.

"Try," he said grimly. "Try to make me understand."

Looking at the fire, she curled her arms around her knees tightly. "I'd never known anyone like you," she said finally. "When I was with you, I felt out of control, intense, passionate." She turned back to him. "Everything was brighter, clearer, more colorful somehow when we were together. It was like being alive for the very first time. Miller, I was scared to death."

"I loved you."

Emotion blurred Natalie's vision. She stared at the fire again and blinked back the tears, determined not to cry. She wasn't finished talking.

"You know that my mother died when I was a baby," she started.

"Yes."

"I don't remember her." She pulled her knees in closer as she continued. "I don't remember anything about her. But I like to think that she loved me, that she must have whispered those words to me at some point when she held me in her arms those few months she lived after I was born. Because after that, no one ever said those words to me again—until you."

Beside her, Miller was very still. "I always thought you were close to your father."

Natalie looked at him, almost laughed.

"My father liked to *keep* me close, but that's not the same thing as *being* close." She shook her head. "All I know about my mother's accident is that she was speeding when it happened, and that it was her fault. Maybe that started it with my father—the overprotection, the rules, the rigid expectations. I don't know. It took me years, but I do believe now that my father loves me. I don't think he's an unfeeling ogre. But he can't express his feelings, and I needed him to, desperately."

"I didn't know," he said quietly. "I guess I thought your life was perfect."

"I guess it looked perfect," she allowed, comforted and tormented by his kindness all at the same time. "How could I complain? I had everything—except what I wanted. And then I met you and you gave it to me so freely, so unconditionally, and I was starving for it. Sometimes, it just seemed too good to be true that you could love me like that. I was very mixed up and insecure. There was only one thing I was sure about—and that was how much I loved you. I never *stopped* loving you."

The crackle of the fire filled the silence between them.

"Then why? Why did you suddenly run away from me?"

Taking the blanket with her, Natalie rose, walked to the hearth, and gazed unseeingly into the dancing flames. She knew when he came up behind her, sensed his tall, powerful presence, longed so much to turn and throw herself into his arms.

She pivoted slowly.

"I was sick," she told him. "I found out that I had cancer."

His face was blank. "You had cancer? But you're healthy; you're—"

"I'm all right now. I've been in remission for eight years."

"Thank God." He stared at her, confusion furrowing his brow. "But you didn't tell me. You never—" He broke off. "Why didn't you tell me?"

His eyes glinted with an emotion that was complicated, unreadable. Dangerous.

"I told myself I was sparing you," she choked out. "But that was a lie, like everything else. I was sick, and it was going to get worse. It was going to be awful, and I knew it. I didn't want you to see me like that. I didn't think—" She couldn't get the rest out over the thick lump in her throat.

Knowledge dawned on his face.

"You didn't think I would want to see you like that," he charged roughly. "You didn't believe I would stand by you."

Regret ripped through her. He *would* have stood by her—she knew that now. She had been so wrong, so completely wrong, but that didn't change anything now, only made it all the more painful.

"I didn't want to be hurt," she whispered. "What I did was wrong. I just didn't—" She took a ragged breath and went on: "I just didn't think you could possibly love me that much—and I couldn't bear to find that out. It was easier to break up with you."

"You didn't give me a chance to love you that much." He spoke with quiet fury.

"No," she agreed miserably. "I didn't give you a chance."

She wanted to run away—run from his intensity, just as she'd done ten years ago. But she couldn't. He deserved to be angry, and she wouldn't take that away from him.

"I hurt you deeply, I know that," she said in a small voice. "You have every right to hate me."

"Natalie, if you think I hate you, you don't know me at all." He gripped her upper arms and hauled her close, and she realized exactly how angry he was. "You're doing it again. Deciding how I feel, and acting on it—without bothering to ask *me.* Damn it, Natalie. Ask me what I'm thinking, what I'm feeling, instead of making it up." He shook her. *"Ask me."*

Their faces were only inches apart. His eyes glittered harshly. She could hear his heart pounding violently, almost feel it.

"Do you hate me?" she whispered over the almost unbearable ache in her chest.

He answered by his mouth crashing down on hers. His kiss was desperate, urgent, yet devastatingly tender, and filled with all the anguish of ten lost years. She had no defenses against it because she knew—*knew*—that he didn't hate her, after all.

He couldn't hate her and kiss her this way. She had felt cold, but his kiss breathed life back into her bones, made her whole and warm. She needed this kiss, needed *him.* Her head swam, her insides hummed, and she could do nothing but cling and kiss him back.

She loved the taste of him, the feel of him. She loved *him.*

When Miller finally broke the kiss, he gazed at Natalie in amazement. She felt so right in his arms, as if she'd never left them, as if those ten long years had been wiped away.

The blanket was slipping down off her shoulders now, and through the terry material of the robe he sensed she was naked. He wanted her, but he knew that both of them needed to take this thing slowly, a step at a time.

"I don't hate you," he murmured softly, because he knew the words had to be said out loud. He had to be sure that she believed him. "I can't

hate you for something you did ten years ago."
He searched her eyes, seeing the awful pain ease
there. "I would have stood by you. I would have
loved you enough."

She pressed her face into his chest, and he
could feel her trembling.

"I know," she whispered. "I'm sorry."

With a light touch, he drew her chin back up
so that she faced him again. "It was my fault, too,"
he admitted. "I should have known something
was wrong that day. You were so hard and cold.
You weren't the Natalie I knew. But I was hurt
and I didn't trust my feelings, so I blocked what
my instincts were telling me. I should have
pushed you until you told me the truth.

"But no one had ever loved me that way before,
either. Everyone I'd ever loved had walked away
from me in the end, and it was easier to believe
that you were like the rest of the world than to
trust my instincts that you were different. We were
both young, both foolish." He paused. "And
we've both grown up."

He held on to her wonderful, lithe body, and
he kissed her again—but this time softly. Healing
her, healing himself.

"The past is gone," he said in a rough, husky
whisper when he released her mouth. "We can't
do anything to change it. It's the future that's in
our hands now, and what we do from this moment
on is what matters."

For all that was so complicated between them,
there was one thing that was simple.

"My heart never left you," he said. "It never forgot you. Never stopped wanting you. Not once in ten years." He took a deep breath. "But I don't want to push you into something you're not ready for. I don't want to scare you again, so we're going to take this slow—"

She threaded her fingers through his hair and drew his lips down to hers. "Please don't take it slow. We've waited too long, wasted too much time." And this time *she* kissed *him*.

It was the most exquisite kiss he'd ever known, and he lost himself in it, savoring every languorous sip of her sheer sweetness. He held her closer, and she melted to him, her curves fitting to his body.

"Make love to me," she whispered when the kiss finally broke.

He saw the desire and need flaring in her eyes, and he knew their bodies were fused too intimately for her not to know the extent of his own arousal as well.

"This is our chance to finish what we started," he said. "To find out where it leads." He paused. Electrical sparks were shooting off all over his body, but there was something he had to hear first. Something he had to know. "I need you to promise me one thing."

She waited.

"Promise me that you won't run, that no matter how things turn out, you won't be so scared of it that you run away without an explanation."

What if his intensity frightened her away again?

He didn't know how to *not* be intense when he was with Natalie. His feelings for her were overwhelming sometimes, even to himself.

"I can't say that I won't be scared," she offered quietly. "But I won't run away."

It was enough. He picked her up lightly, blanket and all.

"Upstairs?" he asked. "Or here?"

She smiled in his arms, glanced at the dancing fire and back at him.

"Here," she said. "Now," she added, laughing. "Anywhere!"

He laughed and placed her on the thick, warm rug before the hearth and settled down beside her. Purposely, cautiously, he kissed her and stroked her, reacquainting himself with her body through the terry material. She smelled like soap and tasted like memories, and he couldn't get enough.

He wanted to be so careful with her, so gentle, but she wasn't patient, and the truth was—he wasn't patient, either. They'd both waited too long for this moment.

Pulling back, he took in the outrageously arousing sight of her lying there—her hair damp and wild, her eyes bright with passion, the blanket tangled beneath her and the terry robe falling open to her sides. Firelight caressed the glimpse of pale ivory skin, transforming it into intriguing swells and secret valleys. Drawing apart the already loosened tie of the robe, she unwrapped herself completely.

"You're so beautiful." He touched her reverently, gliding his fingers over the flat plane of her belly, to the gentle curves of her breasts. He cupped them in his hands, wanting to get to know her all over again. Inch by seductive inch.

"I'm not eighteen anymore," she whispered, and for a moment there was a hint of insecurity in her eyes. "I'm too thin, too—"

He shook his head. "You're perfect." Heat poured into him, just from looking at her, touching her. He was on fire for her, and she was worried that he might find faults, think she was in some way *less* desirable than when she was a teenager? "You're a woman, Natalie, not a girl—and you're exactly what I want."

"You're what I want," she whispered back, her eyes shining.

He groaned and kissed her again, deeper, a wave of tender love rushing over his heart. She *was* his heart, always had been.

She was the one who'd shown him what it was to love, and he'd never stopped loving her.

Finally, starved for air, he let go of her sweet mouth. "There's never been anyone like you for me," he said raggedly. "In all these years, no one has made me feel this way. And God knows, I tried to find someone who could. But there was only you." He pressed hot kisses to her face, her throat, his breathing unsteady, his heart pounding. "Always, only you."

"I haven't—" She stopped, her eyes shimmering. "There's been no one. No one at all."

He blinked, stared at her in amazement. His heart swelled.

"No one?"

She shook her head. "I wasn't—" She bit her lip. "I wasn't trying to be a nun or anything. It's just, I can't make love unless—"

She didn't finish, and he could sense emotion and shyness holding her back.

I love you. Neither of them had said the words aloud, but he felt them in his heart, and he thought she did, too. The love they'd shared long ago had never gone away at all, had only waited to be brought back to life at the right time.

Yet for all that was familiar between them, there was also so much that was new. She wasn't ready, and he wasn't, either, to make big statements. It was easier to show her how he felt, let her show him.

For tonight, it was all they needed.

She reached up to him, pulling him closer. He ducked his head to capture first one nipple, then another, tasting, seducing, nearly dying when she started arching beneath him. They were both shivering—not from cold, but from the extreme emotion of being together again. At the same time, he was feverish, too.

The need was almost painfully intense, and it would have been unbearable if he hadn't been able to see that she felt the same way.

When he reached between them, felt her intimately, he found her waiting for him, slick and soft. Her hands were at his waistband, unsnapping his jeans and tugging at them. He rolled away from her just long enough to tear his pants off and pull his sweatshirt over his head. He came back to her, almost embarrassed by how ready he was for her.

Then the sensation of her skin against his nearly made him mindless. He fused his mouth to her, crushing her soft breasts with his hard chest.

She made little throaty sounds that drove him insane and wrapped her legs around him, urging him into her, all the while kissing and nibbling at his throat, his ears, his mouth.

If she'd been shy a minute ago, she wasn't shy at all now. She was hungry and desperate, just as he was. And for all his desire to take the night slowly, Miller knew this first time together couldn't possibly be anything but an explosion.

He was already dizzy with pleasure and passion, but still he had to think of her.

"I don't want to hurt you," he said, searching her face. "If it's been that long for you since—"

"Don't worry," she whispered, and smiled. "I'm ready." And she reached for him, sweetly, willingly.

It was like coming home. She lifted her hips to meet him, and he moved into her, delicately, and found her not just ready but white hot—and eager. She took him hard and fast, her responsiveness blowing his mind.

It wasn't going to last long, and he wanted to tell her that he needed a second to regain control, that he wanted to draw this out as long as possible, but he couldn't. He couldn't even think, much less speak.

Through the hot haze of wild energy, he saw her throw her head back. Firelight reflected perspiration on her adorable face, and she kissed him, wrapping her arms and legs tighter around his hips while she shattered beneath him.

She cried out against his mouth, and what little control he had left was swept over the edge. He spiraled into that sweet abyss with her.

They stayed that way—tangled and trembling—for hours, maybe days or weeks, or at least it felt that way. In reality, Miller knew it could only have been a few short minutes.

Natalie clung to him as if he was a life raft, and slowly, carefully, he moved to slide next to her. She shifted, and he pulled the blanket out from beneath her, wrapped it over both of them. They snuggled there, both catching their breath, sweating and shivering and staring at each other with awe.

"Do you want to stay here?" he asked finally.

"Oh, yes."

She grinned at him, and he knew he was grinning back.

"I meant, down here in particular," he said. "We could go upstairs, to bed."

"I like here," she said drowsily. "I don't want to move."

She cuddled against him, placing her head in the crook of his shoulder. He gathered her closer, loving the scent of her, the feel of her, everything about her.

He listened to her breathing and knew she slept. He held her, just held her, because he knew as long he did, she would be safe.

FIFTEEN

His kiss was heaven.

Natalie woke to Miller's lips brushing hers. She moaned sleepily, happily, and opened her eyes. He smiled down at her, inches away, his strong face framed by the early morning light filtered softly through the lace-curtained windows.

"Good morning," he said lightly.

Morning. Which came right after night. It all came back to her.

They'd made love. Wild, earth-shaking love. She felt a delirious tingle . . . and a stab of panic. Last night had been the most powerful emotional experience of her life. But what had they started? She wasn't any more certain that she and Miller had a future together now than she had been before.

For all that they'd said last night, there were still things left *unsaid.*

"I hated to wake you," he said. "But I wanted to let you know I'm going out for a while. Plus, I thought you might want to make some calls— your father, your office. I know there are people who're going to be concerned about you this morning. Actually, I thought about calling your father myself rather than waking you, but then I figured hearing from me wouldn't ease his worries much."

He gave her a self-deprecating grin.

It took a massive effort for Natalie to focus. "You're right. I need to call my father." She sat up, belatedly pulling the blanket up with her. *She was naked!* Miller was fully clothed, ready to walk out the door, and that made her feel that much more naked.

The spark in his blue eyes made her feel fluttery and hot, and she knew she was blushing.

"I have a meeting with the fire inspector," he said, still crouched beside her, looking hard, as if he was trying not to laugh at her shy efforts to tug the blanket up to her chin. "I'm going to go over my case notes with him, and hopefully that'll stave off any need for you to make a statement right now—though you may have to make one later."

"Thanks." There were so many things she needed to think about, she realized with a jolt. After she called her father and her office, she needed to contact her insurance agency, start the process of reconstructing her life.

And still, there was someone out there who wanted to hurt her. Here, at Miller's ranch house, that danger seemed far away. But it wasn't, not really. The danger was out there, waiting.

Her stomach knotted. She couldn't hide forever.

"I don't want you to tell anyone where you are," Miller went on quietly, his intense gaze pinning her seriously now. "Promise me. No one. Not even your father."

Natalie swallowed. "My father—"

"Might unknowingly mention to the wrong person where you are," he explained. "Better to be safe than sorry. In fact, if you have a cell phone in your purse, you're probably better off making calls using that."

She nodded. "You're right. I'll be careful, I promise."

"Your clothes are in the dryer, and there's a pot of coffee on the stove." He nodded his head toward the hearth beside them, and she noticed a hand-painted mug with steam rising out of the top. "I brought you a cup to get you started, and I pulled a loaf of bread out of the freezer this morning. There's some jam in the fridge, but that's about it. There's some soup in the cupboard you could heat up for lunch. I'll bring back some supplies this afternoon, and we can talk then about what you're going to do next."

"That's fine. I hate for you to go to so much trouble."

"No trouble." He regarded her. "How are you feeling this morning?"

She chewed her lip, hesitated. "Nervous."

"You're safe here."

She started to get up, dragging the twisted blanket with her, and Miller helped her rise.

"That's not what I mean." She took a few steps to stare out the windows. Soft morning sunshine twinkled over the dewy landscape. Rolling country surrounded them, with nothing and no one as far as she could see.

She turned, looked at Miller. "I'm nervous about us," she admitted. "I'm happy. But I'm nervous."

"Hey." He closed the space between them, slipped his arms around her waist. "I'm nervous, too."

She stared up at him. "Really?"

"Really. We've got a lot to figure out, but we don't have to do it all today. Deal?"

Her heart turned over painfully. "Deal," she whispered.

He kissed her long and hard, and she couldn't bring herself to say anything that might destroy the moment. She didn't know how many moments like this they would have.

Natalie stood back, surveying her handiwork as she brushed an escaping strand from her ponytail out of her eyes. She'd dusted and mopped, and the house practically sparkled.

After Miller left, she'd made a series of phone calls. Her father wanted her to come home, and she told him she'd think about it. She was still worried about placing him in danger, though she didn't explain that to him because she was sure that would only make him worry more. Next, she spoke with Mr. Coleman at the office and arranged personal leave for the rest of the week, then reported to her insurance agency. After that, she'd tried to get in touch with Brad, but in the end had to leave a message with his secretary at the bank.

Then she'd had some toast, showered, dressed in her clothes, and explored the house. It was wonderful—with four bedrooms, a living room and den, a sunroom off the back, a huge, new-looking kitchen that had obviously been remodeled with an enthusiastic cook in mind, and a dining room filled with an incredible collection of antiques.

She'd walked to the barn out of curiosity, and her sense that it had been a working ranch at some point was confirmed, but now the stalls were empty and, like the house, a mournful feeling clung to everything.

Back inside the ranch house, for lack of anything better to do and with the thought of keeping her mind too busy to fret, she dug out cleaning supplies from the walk-in pantry and set to work scrubbing away the melancholy neglect.

She'd gotten more straight hours of sleep last night than any time in the past week, but still she was drooping by the time she was done. A nap, she decided, would be good.

Now, stashing the cleaning supplies back in the pantry, she wrapped herself up in the Indian blanket and lay on the couch. Prissy snuggled up in the crook of her shoulder, and she was almost asleep when her cell phone rang. She had left her purse upstairs and had to run all the way up to Miller's old bedroom for it.

"Brad," she breathed, taking a second to catch her breath. "Hi. I don't know if you saw the news—"

"I did. God. Natalie, are you all right? I had a meeting first thing this morning that I couldn't put off, but as soon as I got your message—"

"I'm fine. I wanted to let you know."

"Where are you?"

Natalie hesitated. She wanted to be honest with Brad, but she knew Miller was right about keeping the situation under wraps. Even Brad might unwittingly tip someone off about her location. It would be burdening him to tell him something he had to keep secret.

"I can't tell you where I am."

"You don't trust me." He sounded hurt, angry.

"No, no. It's for your own protection. Brad, someone set that fire deliberately. Someone burned my house down! I'm safe now, but it's better if you don't know where I am. I'm worried about you. I can't endanger anyone else, not as long as we don't know what's going on."

"You're with Miller." His voice tightened.

"I'm fine. Please don't worry about me."

"I can't help worrying about you, Natalie. We take care of each other. I love you—you know that."

"Oh, Brad." She sat on the edge of Miller's bed, gripping the phone. Brad had been her friend for so long, and he'd gone through so much with her. She hated saddling him with her problems when he was in such personal turmoil of his own now. "I love you, too. But you don't have to take care of me. I'm fine."

"I *want* to take care of you, Nat. I told you, I love you. Don't you get it? *I love you.* You should be here, with me." Something desolate and heart-breaking threaded through his words. "I can take care of you, keep you safe. Marry me, Nat."

"Brad, don't be silly," she said quickly. "We're not even thirty. Besides, thirty's not even that old. Maybe we should up it to forty." She tried to make light of the topic, but she had an awful, sick feeling that Brad was serious. An awful, sick feeling that she was about to lose her best friend.

How had she not seen that his feelings for her were different than hers for him? Guilt wracked her.

"I'm not kidding around," Brad went on, confirming her instincts. "I know we've always joked about this, but somewhere along the line it stopped being a joke for me, Nat. It became real. I love you. Everything that's happened to you lately has made me realize how much you mean to me. I couldn't bear it if anything happened to you. Please, tell me where you are. Let me come get you, take care of you."

Tears misted in her eyes and her throat ached. "I'm sorry, Brad." She didn't know what else to say. She didn't know how to not hurt him. "I can't marry you. I love you, but . . ."

There was an awkward, hurting silence.

"But you don't love me that way," he said, so softly she could scarcely catch the words.

"Brad—"

"I'm sorry, Nat." His voice was clipped and thick. "I've made you uncomfortable. I shouldn't have said anything. Please, forget that this conversation happened."

Before she could speak again, she heard a click that told her he'd hung up. She started to call him back, then stopped. What could she say? Their friendship might not survive this, no matter what she said. There would always be an awkwardness that hadn't been there before.

She went back downstairs to the couch, but she was too miserable and tense to sleep now. What had happened to her boring, peaceful, safe little world? Everything had changed so fast. In her mind, she relived the escalating, frightening events of the past days: the ransacking of her town house, the menacing phone calls, the threatening note with the mouse, the car that had tried to run her down, the late-night break-in at her town house—then the fire that had burned it down. Who could hate her enough to do this? Why?

And what was happening to everyone around her? Ginny was mysteriously missing. Brad was in trouble with his gambling addiction again—and harbored feelings for her that she'd never antici- pated after all the years they'd been friends.

And Miller. Miller was back in her life.

But for how long? Her heart turned over in slow, agonizing increments. She couldn't bear it if she lost him—again.

Miller found her curled up on the couch when he got home. It was strange and wonderful at the same time, coming home to Natalie, but he knew this fantasy domestic scene was only temporary.

With any luck, the case would be solved soon. Even now, the information the neighbors in Natalie's building had given the police and fire inspector had tightened the investigation. The whole matter could be settled very soon.

Then he and Natalie would leave the ranch, go back to their normal lives in Silver City. And then what? They hadn't discussed the future.

While he watched, Natalie opened her eyes, blinking sleepily. She looked startled; then she smiled, instinctively, from the heart.

He set the grocery sacks he carried down on the coffee table and crossed to the couch.

"Hi there." He planted a warm kiss on her mouth.

"Hi," she breathed. She sat up. "Wow. Food, I hope?" She leaned forward to peek in the sacks. "I'm starving. I'm not a great cook, I should tell you that. I'm a nightmare in the kitchen."

"Lucky for you, I'm a master chef." He picked the sacks back up. "Come watch the artist at work," he said teasingly.

She followed him to the kitchen, sat on a stool at the long, barlike counter, looking delicate and messy, her hair tangled, her face clean of makeup. He had more things in the car, and she got up and hugged him when he brought in a dog dish and food for Prissy, and then she flushed hotly when he handed her another bag, this one full of clothes.

"I noticed your size when I put your things in the wash," he said, watching her dig through the bag. "I figured you could wear the sweatshirts and T-shirts from the bureau upstairs, but there are certain other things you'll need."

Natalie pulled out jeans and then underclothes, which she promptly stuffed back down into the bag without looking at him, and then she came to a black lace teddy with red ribbons. She pulled it out, her face so hot he thought she might catch fire.

"You *really* needed that," he said huskily.

She rammed it back into the bag and looked up at him from beneath her thick lashes. "Thanks."

He laughed. "Don't worry," he said. "I won't make you wear it very long." He waggled his brows.

Natalie buried her face in her hands. "I wasn't myself last night," she said softly. "I'm so embarrassed. I'm not a wild woman. I hope you're not going to be disappointed. The truth is, I'm very shy—"

"I love how you were last night," Miller said, gathering her into his arms where she sat on the stool. "You don't have to be embarrassed with me, okay? And there's nothing you can do that would disappoint me."

She lifted her gaze to his face. "I'm new at this, you know."

He nodded, kissed her lightly on the nose. "I know. Actually, I am, too." He set to work cooking, figuring Natalie needed some time to recover her balance. He could use some balance, too. It was easy, too easy, to hold her in his arms and forget everything else. "I noticed what you did with the house today," he said conversationally. He looked back over at her. "Thanks. You didn't have to do that."

"I wanted to keep busy. The house is beautiful. And so huge! I walked out to the barn. What was it like when John and Emily were here? Looks like it used to be a working ranch."

Miller nodded. He finished putting the newly purchased supplies away in the pantry and started cleaning two potatoes for dinner.

"They bought the place to retire—though of course John would never have really retired. They both loved the West, and everything about it. I'm sure you can tell from the collectibles around the house."

Natalie nodded.

He wrapped the potatoes in foil and slid them into the oven to bake. After setting out lettuce, tomatoes, and mushrooms, he reached for the cutting board.

Natalie got up and came over. "I can do that," she said. "I can't burn salad," she teased.

Miller gave her the cutting board and the knife, and they worked side by side. She watched, amazed, while he made biscuits from scratch.

"Emily," he said in response to Natalie's gaping expression. "She worked me hard when I came to live with them. She and John both. John had just started stocking the ranch with a few horses, a few head of cattle. He'd already cut back at the station, planning to retire within a few years. He had me out there at dawn with a hammer and nails, building that barn with him. And at night, Emily made me help her with dinner. And not just easy stuff, like setting the table. She made me learn to cook, from scratch. Between the two of them, they didn't leave me any time for feeling sorry for myself, and they made damn sure I got motivated pretty quickly and figured out something to do with my life—or else I knew I'd be making biscuits and mending fences for the rest of my days. And that was hard work! But I knew they cared about me, and that's what made all the difference."

Natalie laughed. "They sound wonderful. I'm envious, actually."

Miller looked at her. "I was lucky, really lucky. I wanted to be just like John, and he couldn't have been prouder when I announced I wanted to go to the police academy."

They continued to work for several minutes, quietly. Miller wanted to tell Natalie about what was going on with the case, but she was relaxed now, and he hated to spoil her chance to have a normal evening. At least for a little while.

"What are you going to do with the ranch?" she asked later, when the salad was fixed and the steaks were broiling. They sat at the polished oak kitchen table with glasses of white zinfandel.

Miller stared at the spacious kitchen, the heart of the house when Emily had been here. "I don't know," he admitted. "When they died, I sold off the stock. I couldn't keep the ranch going, working full-time in Silver City. I had my apartment there, and I wasn't comfortable moving out here alone. But I couldn't bring myself to sell it, either." He paused. "I guess I thought it would be a great place to raise a family someday."

He saw something unreadable pass over Natalie's face. "Yes," she said softly. "It would." She stared out the window at the dusky landscape, fingering the stem of the wineglass.

He wanted to know what she was thinking, but he didn't ask. Natalie's thoughts were her own, and he had no right to force them from her. If she needed time, he would give it to her.

But for now, there was something he had to tell her, and he couldn't put it off anymore.

"The preliminary investigation into the fire at your building suggests that accelerants were involved," he said. "A warrant's been issued for Ethan Parrish's arrest."

Natalie gasped. "Ethan?"

"One of your neighbors got a good look at the person who was skulking around your town house right before the fire started, caught him dead-on with his flashlight through his back window. I realized when I went over the statements this morning that his description matched Parrish's. I was able to contact your neighbor where he's staying with some family, and talk to him again. There was a police photo of Parrish from his arrest in Arkansas, and I had that faxed here today. It's old, but the face hasn't changed much. The neighbor identified him."

"But why would Ethan set fire to my town house?"

Miller shook his head. "We don't know that yet. The layoff? It's possible. Or it could be some other twisted reason only Parrish understands. If we could bring him in, maybe we could find out. We've been in touch with the police in Arkansas. If he shows up in his hometown, they'll get him. And we're on alert here. One way or another, he'll be found. And as soon as he is, you'll be safe."

"Safe," Natalie whispered. Hope filled her chest.

They ate dinner, talking quietly. Miller didn't bring up the investigation again, and Natalie was glad. She didn't want to think about it.

She wanted to pretend that she and Miller were just two normal people, in a normal romantic relationship, finding out about each other and exploring the possibilities without so much confusion and darkness hanging over and between them.

She put on the black teddy and he held true to his word that he wouldn't let her wear it very long. It was across the bedroom in under thirty seconds, but from that moment on, the evening slipped into ultraslow motion as he picked her up and placed her gently, so gently, on the bed. Miller pulled his shirt over his head, then dropped the rest of his things in a heap on the floor before joining her beneath the covers.

"Last night was . . ." Miller's voice trailed off for a moment. "Amazing," he said finally. "I don't know how else to describe it. There aren't words. But it was too fast. It was too—"

She stopped his words with a kiss. "It was wonderful," she whispered.

He groaned, pulled her close, and kissed her slowly, completely. It promised all the sweetness of their lovemaking from the night before, and something more. Something deliberate and thought-out.

Knowing hands skimmed over her, leaving tingling throbs all over her body. It might have been scary, how much she needed him—except it was so obvious how much he needed her back.

She ached for him to be inside her, but he held back. He kissed her face, her chin, her neck. Instinctively, she began pushing her hips against his hard arousal, tormented by desire—but still he kissed her and touched her and just held her so incredibly tenderly that it brought tears to her eyes. Then he pushed his fingers inside her, and she burned white hot.

It was the sweetest torment she'd ever known.

Her voice barely worked. "Please," she finally begged.

"Tell me what you want," he whispered back. "You're in control, sweetheart."

His voice was rough, sexy, unbearably arousing. "I want you," she said demandingly, arching beneath him. She fisted her hands in his hair. "Now."

He let out a laughing moan as he gazed down at her, his eyes hungry and hot.

"You want this?" he asked, placing his mouth on one tight nipple and sucking.

"Yes," she breathed wildly.

"And this?" He dragged his mouth across her chest to the other nipple.

She nearly died. And then slowly, so slowly, he lowered his hardness into her, and she went to heaven.

"Yes, yes, yes," she whispered over and over.

It was great, beyond fantastic, far past any thought she was capable of forming in her mind. Her hips rose to meet his, and it was she who speeded it up, desperately needy with a helpless urgency she couldn't control.

She exploded, over and over, whimpering and dazzled. And still there was more, tiny shatterings, one after another, until finally, with her legs tightly gripped around him, he followed into that sweet surrender.

* * *

"Wake up!"

Natalie poked Miller in the shoulder.

He blinked blearily. "What?"

"The phone," she said, nudging him gently again. "The phone's ringing. Your phone. I'm not sure I should get it."

Miller shook off the cobwebs of sleep and jerked to full consciousness. They were tangled up in the sheets in his room, pale gray light filtering in through the narrow window.

The phone shrilled again from the bedstand. He grabbed it. Natalie was unable to keep from staring at his incredible nude body. His hair was adorably rumpled, which did nothing to diminish his sexuality.

She wanted him to get rid of whoever was on the phone and put his wonderful, seductive hands and his hot, magical mouth back on her body. *She really was turning into a wanton!*

Miller put the phone down and looked at her.

His expression scared her, slicing into the cocoon of sensual serenity left over from the night before.

"What is it?" A horrible shiver prickled all the way up her spine.

"That was a buddy of mine at the department. They pulled a body out of Silver Lake early this morning."

She started feeling nauseous. She knew from his voice that something awful was coming.

"A drowning?" Her words sounded faraway, not her own.

Miller shook his head. "A shooting victim. Probably dead before the body hit the water."

He paused. Goosebumps rose on Natalie's arms.

"The body's been identified. It's Ethan Parrish."

SIXTEEN

"I want you to stay here."

Miller's eyes were cool, dangerous, and unnerving even though the fury in them wasn't directed at Natalie. She knew the fury was directed at whoever was behind the continuing bizarre chain of incidents that had begun with the ransacking of her town house a week ago.

It had only been a week ago. To Natalie, it felt like forever.

Her life had changed that much.

She sat up in bed in Miller's room, the sheet still tangled around her body, watching him. He'd dressed in his crisp uniform, slung on his holstered weapon. Tension hummed through her veins at a steady, painful pace.

"No one knows you're here," he went on. "And as long as that's true, you're safe. If you make any phone calls, use your cellular. Keep the house locked. Don't open the door if anyone shows up. No one *should* show up—so there's something wrong if they do. Call me if anything strange happens. If Parrish's death is connected to the arson, then he wasn't acting alone. We don't know who else might be involved, and until we do, we're going on the assumption that you're still in danger."

He went to the closet, reached up to the top shelf and brought down a locked box. Using a key, he opened it and took out a revolver. He commenced loading it.

"What are you doing?"

"I want you to have something for protection."

She stared at it uncomfortably. "I've never used a gun in my life."

Miller sat on the bed beside Natalie.

"It's really not complicated." He demonstrated how to cock it. "Point and pull the trigger," he said. "That's it."

He rose, and she followed him downstairs. At the door, he turned, his gaze searing into her.

"I don't want to leave you." He took her face in his hands and kissed her hard. "But I'm going to find out who's doing this—and I'm going to stop them."

Natalie shut the door behind him, and not for the first time wondered how this could be happening to her.

She went upstairs and stared at the gun sitting on the bedstand where Miller had left it. Would she have the courage to use it? She didn't want to find out.

Her purse was sitting on top of the bureau now, so she put the gun inside it just so she wouldn't have to look at it.

The silence of the house around her seeped into her consciousness. It was nerve-wrackingly quiet without Miller there.

As she showered, she thought over and over of everything Ginny had ever said about Ethan Parrish, and she worried again about Ginny. Had Ethan done something terrible to her?

And who had shot Ethan? She couldn't remember Ginny mentioning any friends that she and Ethan associated with, and she'd always had the impression that Ethan was something of a loner.

Was Ethan's death connected to her case, or was it completely unrelated?

The only thing that seemed certain was that Ethan had set fire to her building, and even that stretched her credulity. How could Ethan hate her that much? She examined in her mind the few times she'd met him, and could remember nothing about the incidents that would foreshadow this chain of events.

When she got out of the shower, she toweled her hair dry and dressed in the clothes Miller had bought for her. She looked around at the clean house and wondered how she was going to fill the hours till his return.

The Silver Lake Campground was usually quiet on spring mornings during the week, but not today. The road into the campground was lined with cars. Police officers, media people, and curiosity-seekers crowded the area. Yellow crime scene tape blocked off a large zone adjacent to the discovery of Parrish's body.

Miller watched a lab specialist mix plaster with water, then pour it into a frame. Several well-defined shoe prints in the soft mud at the edge of lake were being preserved. A fisherman had discovered Parrish's body where it had been dumped in the thick grassy marsh of the lakeshore. The body had already been removed by the coroner's office, and it was only the faxed police photo of Parrish from Arkansas the day before that had led to his immediate identification. One of the officers responding to the scene had seen the photo come in.

The immediate identification and the shoe prints were the first strikes of luck in the week since this madness had begun. If, Miller reminded himself, Parrish's death was indeed connected to Natalie's case.

Still, without a suspect, there wasn't anyone to match the shoe prints to.

He experienced an overwhelming burn of frustration as he drove back to the station. Sitting at his desk, he pulled out the notebook in which he'd kept records on Natalie's case. He flipped through the pages, rereading interviews and case notes on the investigation before turning back to one of the early pages, where he'd listed the names of all the laid-off employees from Universal Technologies. He'd have to check back with each one of them, verify their whereabouts, interview them regarding Parrish's murder.

But Universal Technologies was only one link between Natalie and Ethan Parrish. Ginny was another. Where was she?

He'd started looking into Ginny's disappearance on Monday, but his efforts had been interrupted yesterday by the arson investigation. Flipping forward in the book, he looked at his notes on the Coleman and Brock receptionist. A couple of hours canvassing Ginny's apartment complex had added up to zero in the sum total of his knowledge. Apparently, Ginny lived quietly, talking to few of her neighbors.

He unfolded the sheet of paper tucked between the pages. It was a photocopy of Ginny's lease agreement, provided by the apartment manager. As references, Ginny had listed her parents, Frank and Angela Moore. The address entered was San Paulo, Texas, a scrap of a town near the U.S.-Mexican border.

He hadn't gotten an answer when he'd tried the number the day before. Picking up the receiver from the phone on his desk, Miller jabbed the number in again. The phone rang six times. He was about to hang up when a woman answered.

"Mrs. Moore?" he asked.

"You have the wrong number." The voice held a thick Spanish accent.

The phone clicked.

Miller frowned, jabbed the number in once more.

"This is Officer Miller Brannigan with the Silver

City Police Department. I'm looking for Frank or Angela Moore." Miller reeled off the number.

"I've had this number for three years," the woman said. She supplied Miller with her name and address. "There is no Frank or Angela Moore here, and I've never heard of them."

"Have you ever heard of Ginny Moore?"

"No." She hung up.

Miller tried information for San Paulo, but there were no Moores listed. He picked up the phone again a minute later to call the cell phone number that Natalie had given him.

Her voice was warm and soft, and he wanted to go home right then and put his arms around her. She made him feel good, even from miles away.

"Any news?" she asked.

"Not much," he said honestly. "Nat, I'm trying to find Ginny. I tried to call her parents in San Paulo, and the number she listed on her lease agreement doesn't pan out. Do you know if her parents have moved? Do you have any information about them at all that would help me trace them?"

"I can't think of anything. I wish I could. I'm so worried about her."

"Have you thought of anything that would explain why Ethan Parrish would set fire to your building, other than his connection to Universal Technologies?"

"No," she said firmly. "Nothing."

"What about anyone else, anyone connected to Ethan and Ginny?"

"I've been wracking my brain all morning, and I can't think of anyone Ginny ever mentioned, friends of theirs, or anything. Ginny was shy, kept to herself. I don't know if she had any close friends other than me."

She sounded stressed, and Miller hated grilling her.

"All right. But listen, if you think of anything at all—about Ginny or anyone else—let me know. Anything different or new about anyone around you could be important, even if it doesn't *seem* important on the surface."

She hesitated. "Well, I haven't mentioned this because it's private, but I know that you're aware of Brad's trips to Las Vegas. He told me about your visit to his office on Monday. But I'm not sure if you realize he's an addict. Gambling is like a drug to him. He was in treatment years ago, and I thought he'd overcome it—but he hasn't. He's been gambling again."

"I suspected as much," Miller said.

After finding out about Brad's recent frequent trips to Vegas in his private plane, he'd had a friend at the station run some off-the-record computer checks on Brad, but he hadn't come up with anything that suggested recent financial trouble from gambling debts. And even if he had, he wasn't sure what the connection would have been to Natalie's case, if any.

He felt as if he was grasping at straws—and still coming up empty.

There was a short silence.

"There's something else," Natalie said. "He proposed to me yesterday."

Miller's gut clenched. "He what?"

"He proposed. Well, we've had a sort of running joke between us about this proposal," she rushed on. "It wasn't serious, but yesterday Brad *was* serious. It was kind of horrible, actually. I had to tell him that I could never feel that way about him. It was a shock. I've always cared for Brad, loved him even, but not like that."

"I'm glad to hear it," Miller couldn't help saying.

Natalie was quiet for a minute.

"Yeah?"

"Yeah," he said. "Don't you know—" No, he thought. She couldn't know. He hadn't told Natalie how deeply he felt, and he suddenly wondered what he was waiting for. He loved her, and life was too short and too precarious to let his fear of losing her again get in the way.

He sensed she was afraid for some reason, too. But whatever it was, they had to get it out in the open and deal with it. Tonight.

He had to find out if they had a real chance at a future together.

"Listen, we need to talk," he said. "Really talk—about us, where we're heading."

"I know," she said softly.

"I'll be home in a few hours."

After he hung up, Miller stared at the phone, thinking over Natalie's words. He felt an uncomfortable mix of irritation and relief. The fact was, he was glad Brad Harrison was out of Natalie's life.

There was something about Brad that made him uncomfortable, always had, but was it anything more than jealousy?

He flipped through his notebook and found his interview with the minister's wife from the condominium next door to Brad's. The quote he was looking for leaped out at him.

Miller reached for the phone again. "Mrs. Blakeley?"

Natalie nearly jumped out of her skin when her cell phone rang the instant she set it back down.

"Miller?" she said automatically, thinking he was calling her back.

"It's me. Ginny."

Natalie gasped. "Ginny. Where are you?"

"At a convenience store, out on Highway 54 South," Ginny said. "I don't know what to do." She burst into tears.

"Ginny! What's wrong?"

"Everything," Ginny choked out. "I'm out of money. I've been living in my car. I'm almost out of gas, and I don't know what I'm going to do next."

"Why are you living in your car? Ginny, why did you disappear? I've been worrying about you."

"It's Ethan. He came to my apartment and I thought he was going to kill me. And now *he's* dead." She sounded hysterical. "I was just sitting here, and it came on the radio. Someone murdered him! I'm so terrified, Nat!"

"Oh, Ginny. Surely you don't have anything to be afraid of." Natalie stopped. She really couldn't tell Ginny that. If Ethan's death *wasn't* related to her own case, there could be something else Ethan had been involved in that might be placing Ginny in danger. And whatever the truth was, it was clear that Ginny was in a panic at this point. "Have you been in touch with your family?" she asked, recalling what Miller had told her about trying to track down Ginny's parents. If there was ever a time Ginny needed her family, it was now.

Ginny burst into fresh sobs. "I don't have any family."

"What?" Natalie sat back on the couch, shocked.

She was downstairs in the living room. Prissy scampered across the floor to climb into her lap, her little nails clicking on the hardwood floor.

"I lied. I lied about everything. My dad ran out on us when I was ten, and my mother kicked me out when I was seventeen. I don't know why. I just couldn't tell you that, so I made up this thing about my big, close family. The truth was embarrassing. Your life was so perfect, and mine was so—"

"Oh, Ginny. You know my life isn't perfect."

"It doesn't matter now."

"Yes, it does," Natalie said firmly. "It matters if you don't have anywhere to go."

Ginny let out a cry that sounded strangled, as

if she pressed her hand over her mouth. "I don't know what I'm going to do."

"I want you to—" Natalie hesitated. *I want you to come here.* How could she let Ginny come to the ranch? She would be breaking her promise to Miller not to let anyone know where she was.

But how could she *not* let Ginny come to the ranch? Ginny had been her friend for too long for Natalie to abandon her now. She couldn't leave Ginny alone and terrified on the side of the highway.

She wished desperately for her car, still parked on the street near her burned-out town house.

"Can you go to the police station? Miller is there and—"

"No!" Ginny half-sobbed, half-whispered. "I have to hide, Nat. I just—I have to hide somewhere." She cried softly. "Don't worry about me. I'll be fine. I have to go. I'm sorry. I shouldn't have called you."

"Wait." Natalie decided quickly, tension coiling in her chest. "You have to come here—that's all there is to it." She gave Ginny directions to the ranch house. "We'll talk, figure something out when you get here, all right? Everything's going to be okay."

She clicked the END button on her cell phone, then walked with it to the kitchen. Miller had left the police station number on a pad on the counter. She punched in the number to the station house.

The assistant to the desk sergeant who picked

up the phone identified himself as Officer Calloway. He told her that Miller was on another line, and agreed to take a message for him.

"This is Natalie Buchanan. Tell him Ginny called me. She heard about Ethan's murder on the radio and she's scared, so I'm letting her come out to the ranch house. Thanks."

She hung up, her mind moving ahead to the locked ranch gate. Grabbing the extra set of keys from the hook inside the pantry door, she remembered her purse and the gun. It felt paranoid to take it with her to walk up the driveway, but she ran upstairs anyway.

It was strange to be outside now, as if she were an escaping prisoner. The heavy weight of the gun inside her purse wasn't making her feel any better.

Don't be silly, she told herself, shaking off the eerie feeling.

The day was bright, if slightly breezy, and she started walking in the sunshine down the drive to the gate.

She was almost there when the dark sedan pulled straight in, stopping in front of the barred metal entrance. A memory from the night outside the hospital flashed in Natalie's mind. The dark car roaring toward her.

Her stomach rolled. She stared at the sedan. The driver's side door opened and Ginny climbed out, waved, and Natalie felt completely foolish.

She picked up her pace, eagerness and relief at seeing Ginny whole and healthy filling her heart. As she got closer, she noticed that Ginny had lost weight this past week, too, and the familiar oversize sweater she wore so often to the office flapped more loosely than usual around her delicate body.

The car's windows were shaded with dark sun protection, but from what she could see, the backseat was packed—with hanging clothes and mounds of blankets and bags. Natalie felt sick to think of Ginny living in the cramped vehicle for days on end.

They met at the gate, throwing their arms around each other over the waist-high metal barrier. "Thank God you're all right," Natalie breathed.

"Nat. I'm so glad to see you," Ginny whispered, her voice thick. When she pulled away, Natalie saw that she was crying.

"Come on. We're getting you inside. I'll fix some soup and we'll talk. And you'll be safe." Natalie hugged her again; then Ginny stood back and Natalie climbed easily over the gate. She fiddled with the padlock and the keys till she fit the right one into the lock and swung open the gate.

Ginny went around to the driver's side. She looked at Natalie over the top of the car, her eyes haunted and miserable.

"Maybe you should walk up to the house," she said. "My car's really packed. It won't be comfortable."

Her voice sounded strange, and her skin had turned pasty.

Natalie shook her head. "I don't mind. Besides, I don't want to leave you alone. Don't worry about it."

She was afraid Ginny was going to faint before she could pull the car up to the house. She waited till Ginny drove through the entrance and stopped the car again; then Natalie relocked the gate, dropped the keys into her purse, and opened the front passenger door to get in. Sliding inside, she shoved over a small box to make more room at the same time she dropped her purse on the floor between her feet.

She didn't know what surprised her more when she turned: the fact that Brad had appeared out of nowhere from the backseat, or that he was holding the business end of a pistol against her head.

"Hello, Nat," he said.

SEVENTEEN

Miller put down the phone. Across the crowded office, the assistant to the desk sergeant made eye contact and waved a slip of paper at him while he took another call. The buzz of voices and the harsh scent of burned coffee seemed to add to the tension that was gathering like a hard knot in his gut.

He got up and took the note from the rookie officer.

"When did this come in?" he demanded as soon as Calloway finished his call.

"A few minutes ago, sir. You were on the phone."

"You wrote down precisely what she said?" he probed tersely. "These are her exact words?"

Calloway took the message slip back and studied it. "Natalie Buchanan said to tell you Ginny called her. Ginny heard about Ethan's murder on the radio and she's scared, so she's letting her come out to the ranch house. That's what she said." He looked nervous. "She's talking about that Parrish guy, right?"

Miller pivoted without answering, headed at a fast clip down the hall to the front of the building. He zeroed in on the senior officer at the information desk.

"Has the name of the victim pulled out of Silver Lake this morning been released to the media?"

The sergeant shook his head. "Waiting on notification of next of kin."

He wasn't even finished speaking before Miller was reaching over his desk for his phone. He jabbed in Natalie's cellular number, swearing at the same time. No answer.

"Something wrong?" the sergeant asked.

Miller was already gone.

"I'm sorry," Ginny whimpered. She looked imploringly at Natalie from the driver's seat. "I'm so sorry. I love you, Nat. But I love him, too. I can't help it. You know I've never had anybody, been anybody. With Brad, I have that chance. A chance at the kind of life I've never—"

"Shut up, Ginny." Brad's voice was low and menacing, as Natalie had never heard it before. "We'll need your keys, Nat. Ginny, get her purse."

Natalie watched in horror as Ginny picked up her purse and started handing it over the backseat to Brad. Her thoughts swerved wildly to the gun inside, and an automatic instinct instilled by Miller's crime survival course took over.

React, resist. Don't wait for the perfect chance to escape.

She made a grab for the purse. She never even saw Brad move, just felt the crack on the side of her head. Stars danced in her vision and she slammed back against the passenger door in sharp, stunning pain.

"I'm in a bad mood today, Nat. I'd appreciate a little cooperation."

Sobs filled the cramped interior of the car, and it took Natalie timeless beats to figure out that they were coming from Ginny. Ringing filled her ears and she tasted blood. She realized that she'd bit her tongue when he'd smacked her with the gun.

She stared dazedly at Brad as he pulled the revolver out of her purse with his free hand.

"Well, well." His gaze snapped quickly back to her. "I didn't know you were carrying now, Nat. I suppose this must be Brannigan's influence." Her gun disappeared into the backseat while he kept his own weapon firmly lodged against her temple. Next, he pulled out the heavy key ring she'd taken from the ranch house pantry. "Unlock the gate." He tossed the keys at Ginny. "Sorry to go through this little routine, Nat, but I thought it would be nicer to wait till you got into the car on your own. I didn't want to rough you up to get you in here. Of course, now you've made me rough you up, anyway. I really don't enjoy that. Please don't make me have to do it again."

"What are you doing?" she demanded in a startled whisper.

"I'm doing what you forced me to do," Brad said. He flicked a swift glance at Ginny. "Hurry up. I want to get out of here."

Ginny's whimpers hitched pitifully as she obeyed. She turned the car off, then opened and shut the driver's side door. Natalie kept her eyes on Brad, using the pain in her head as an anchor to focus on his hard face. She was afraid that if she didn't focus on something, she'd black out. Her head was still swimming and she felt like throwing up.

"What am I forcing you to do?"

"You should have come to me. You needed me. You were scared. You were supposed to turn to me, Nat. But you turned to Brannigan, didn't you?"

Natalie swallowed thickly. "You did all those things to scare me? So I would turn to you?" she breathed. "You ransacked my house, sent me that mouse, tried to run me down? Broke my window? The phone calls? The fire? What about the fire?" Confusion wracked her. *Ethan* had set the fire. Hadn't he?

Brad's eyes lit with amusement. "Of course I didn't do all that. I didn't do any of it—that's the beauty of it. Ethan was useful. For a time."

Natalie blinked. "I don't understand. Ethan and Ginny—"

"Ethan was an idiot. Ginny helped me pick him out. Their relationship was a front—that's all—

but he kept forgetting that. He had a hard time drawing the line between business and personal. He went berserk when he realized Ginny wasn't really going to fall in love with him. Getting paid wasn't enough for him. He wanted Ginny, too. That's where he made his mistake. He didn't respect what was mine."

"You killed Ethan," Natalie gasped.

Brad's eyes were cold. "He gave me no choice."

The driver's side door opened and Ginny slid back in.

"Back the car out," Brad instructed. "Then get out and lock the gate again. We want to leave everything looking normal."

Ginny started the car and the vehicle crept backward through the ranch entrance. Then she turned it off and got back out to lock the gate. For the seconds the car door was open, Brad used his other arm to reach up and grip Natalie's upper arm, as if worried she might dive out after Ginny, despite the gun at her head.

Would he really shoot her if she tried to lunge out of the car the next time Ginny opened the door?

Something else from the crime survival class sprang into her consciousness. *Expect to be hurt.* She couldn't let fear stop her.

She'd already let too many chances for happiness slip through her fingers because of fear, and she wasn't letting Brad take this last chance away from her. She was going to live, and she was going to tell Miller the whole truth this time—and she was going to pray that he would love her when she did. But to find out, to have that chance, she had to live.

From the edge of her vision, she looked for Ginny. She could see her fumbling at the lock, having some kind of problem. Ginny's whole body was trembling, so she figured her hands were no better.

Her gaze moved to Brad. She had to keep him talking, distract him, and maybe if she understood what was going on, there would be some way she could talk him out of whatever crazy scheme he was attempting to perpetrate.

"If you and Ginny—" She was still having trouble digesting the idea that Brad and Ginny were involved in a romantic relationship. "Why would you want to marry me if you and Ginny—"

"I got in trouble with bookies, big trouble. These are the kind of people who break your legs, or worse, if you don't pay. I borrowed from the bank—to use the term loosely—to pay them off. Got them off my back last weekend. But now the bank's on my back. My father's already suspicious, talking about bringing in outside auditors. I can fix the accounts I stole from—but I have to have the money. And I can't wait any longer."

"Why didn't you just ask me for a loan?"

Brad laughed, and the sound chilled her.

"It's not that kind of money, Nat. You don't borrow half a million dollars from a friend, now do you? But my wife would share without even knowing it. As your loving husband, a financial professional, I would have been happy to take over management of your fiscal affairs."

"I don't have half a million dollars," she said, shocked.

"You have a trust fund."

"There was only twenty-five thousand dollars in my trust fund, Brad." It was something her mother had left to her, which came to her on her twenty-first birthday. She'd used it as the down payment on the town house.

She felt a hysterical bubble rise up her throat at the realization that Brad had come after her for something she didn't even possess. And she felt sick as it dawned on her that if she *had* married Brad, her life as Mrs. Brad Harrison would likely have been a short one.

As soon as he'd gotten control of her money— what money she had, anyway—he would have been finished with her. What had he planned for her? A nice little accident? Her mind reeled with the pain of betrayal.

"Twenty-five thousand dollars?" Brad repeated after her. A furious gleam lit his eyes, but his controlled facade didn't change. "Well, then, things always turn out for the best, don't they?" His voice was terrifyingly cool. "We're on Plan B now. Your father has half a million dollars twenty times over or more, and I'm sure when he finds out you're in danger, he'll be happy to fork it over."

Natalie was so stunned that she forgot to watch

for Ginny. The former receptionist was in the driver's seat again before she realized it.

"You're holding me for ransom?" Despair rolled over her in icy waves. Not only had she missed a chance to escape, but she was completely convinced that Brad was insane. "You'll never get away with it."

"I will." He flicked a glance at Ginny, who was cowering in the driver's seat. "Drive," he ordered. He looked back at Natalie. "I'm going to let you live for a while. I need you to play the terrified hostage on the phone to your father. But since Ethan had to leave our team unexpectedly, I don't have anyone to watch you—so I'll have to stash you tied up, alone. It won't be comfortable, but I can't help that. I'm afraid I can't trust Ginny with the job of supervising you. She's a little weak where you're concerned."

Ginny broke into another round of sniffling sobs, but she started up the engine obediently, began backing the rest of the way out of the driveway.

Brad drew a tape recorder out of his pocket. "I would consider it a real favor to me if you'd record a little message for your dear father. You can tell him you're fine, and that if he follows instructions, you'll be returned safely. Now, if you don't want to do the favor for me, how about doing it for your dad? I'm sure it'll make him feel good to hear from you. You don't want to deprive him of this opportunity to hear your sweet voice, do you? Take a few minutes to think about it. We'll

pull over and take care of it when we get somewhere safe."

Somewhere safe. Natalie had a feeling the next
place they pulled over was going to be the *last*
place she ever pulled over.

Ginny turned the car out of the ranch driveway
and onto the farm-to-market road that cut across
the rolling countryside. They headed toward
Highway 54.

Natalie's heart banged against the wall of her
chest. *He was going to kill her.* He'd have to, to get
away with it.

"Do you mind if I put my seat belt on?" she
asked quietly, thinking ahead desperately to the
only choice she had left. Adrenaline burned down
her veins.

Brad looked amused. "Of course. Go right
ahead."

Natalie reached slowly, carefully, for the shoulder belt, latching it securely in place before
straightening again. She could still feel the cold
nose of Brad's gun at her head.

The road ahead was vacant. Fence posts whizzed
by, framed by empty land stretching away on both
sides. They came up over a rise, and her gaze
fixed on a massive oak tree on the opposite side
of the road.

"Drive faster, Ginny," Brad demanded. "But
don't speed after we get on the highway." He
looked down for a second, and she heard the rus-
tle of a map. "I want you to—"

Natalie lunged at the steering wheel, grabbed

it, and twisted. The sound of Ginny's screams filled the car just before they plowed into the tree.

Miller pushed eighty, then ninety, as his cruiser ate up the miles down Highway 54. He turned off on the farm-to-market road that led to the ranch house, impatiently adjusting his speed for the narrow, curved road that sliced into the rugged countryside. His police scanner kept up an erratic, squawking accompaniment.

Tension radiated to every nerve end of his body. *He couldn't lose Natalie, not now.*

After she'd told him about Brad's proposal, he'd phoned Mrs. Blakeley again to question her more closely about Brad's regular overnight female guest. Brad's declaration of love for Natalie gave him a bad feeling, and he had to find out if it was more than personal. What he'd found out was that the description of Brad's lover matched Ginny's.

Ginny, who knew more about the body pulled out of Silver Lake this morning than had been released to the press.

He was still unclear about what it all meant, but knowing that Ginny was on her way to the ranch house was enough for him.

The cruiser swooped down through a thick, wooded hollow that hugged a creekbed, then up and around a curved hill to a half-mile expanse of flat road framed by pastureland.

He spotted the crashed sedan the second he came up over the rise. The hood was crumpled like an accordion, the back hanging off over the culvert between the road and the tree. Reaching instinctively for the handheld radio, he called for an ambulance.

Everything happened in the space of a heartbeat. The front passenger door of the sedan pushed open and a woman stumbled out. Natalie's long blond hair flew in the light spring breeze. The back door opened and a man staggered forward. He whipped around to see Miller's cruiser bearing down on the crash site, then tore after Natalie, tackling her to the ground.

He had a gun in his hand.

Years of experience and training kept Miller steady, kept him from exploding into anguished fury. Radio still in his fist, he called for backup, then jammed his foot to the gas pedal, roaring up to the wreckage and screeching to a halt.

He flew out of the car, gun drawn, and came to a stunning stop at the edge of the culvert. Brad had Natalie in a stranglehold on the ground, his pistol stabbing at the side of her head.

Desperation choked the air.

"Drop your gun, Brannigan," Brad ordered.

"No, Miller—" Natalie started, and his gut twisted when she ended on a suffocated cry of pain as Brad tightened his hold on her neck.

Miller took a deep breath, forcing icy calm, control. He had to be in control, or he could lose her.

"I already called for backup, Brad," Miller said quietly, evenly. He lowered his gun to a non-threatening position but didn't drop it. "They'll be here soon. You don't want to add murder to your list of crimes."

Brad laughed harshly.

"Murder's already on my list of crimes. Ask Parrish."

His voice was sharp, raspy. Miller guessed he'd suffered internal injuries, and that it was sheer force of will that carried the man.

A will that could kill Natalie.

"You can't get away with this, Brad."

"I can, and I will. I have your car, and I have Nat." He lurched to a stand, dragging Natalie up with him. "My very own police car. Who'd have thought it? I'm sure you won't mind riding in the trunk—if you care about what happens to our Nat, that is. My plane's ready and waiting at the airport. We'll be crossing the Rio Grande before anyone starts looking for you. Now, if you'll put your gun on the ground, we can get started. Or would you rather I blow Nat's pretty head off? Trust me, Brannigan, I've got less to lose all the time. If your backup arrives and I don't have a hope in hell of getting out of here, I'll shoot myself. I won't go to prison—I can promise you that. And I promise you I won't go down alone, either. I'll shoot Nat first, then myself. But if you help me get out of here, I'll take Nat with me."

"Don't do it, Miller," Natalie cried. "If you do what he says, he'll kill you. Don't you dare get yourself shot over me—"

Brad jerked his arm hard against her throat and she gasped sharply. "Let's go, Brannigan," he demanded. "If you want Nat to live to see tomorrow, you'll—"

"No!"

Miller's gaze darted to the other side of the crashed vehicle. Ginny limped around the car, her face ashen, blood streaming into her eyes. He recognized his revolver in her hand.

Her aim trembled as she pointed it at Brad.

"This has to stop," she cried. "I can't let you do this. It's gone too far. It wasn't supposed to be like this! It was enough that you killed Ethan. You're not going to hurt Natalie anymore. Or Miller. You can't keep killing people!"

"Don't be stupid, Ginny," Brad snapped nastily. "Put the gun down. Or hell, do something useful—shoot Brannigan."

"No." Ginny fumbled with the weapon.

"You can't even cock it, Ginny. Put it down."

The quiet click of the gun cocking broke through the air.

The gun shook in Ginny's hand.

"Put the gun down, Brad, or I'll shoot you. I swear I will."

Brad took the pistol off Natalie's head and swung his arm around to level his aim at Ginny.

In the exact moment that Natalie tore from Brad's hold and threw herself off to the right, Miller lifted his gun. Brad jerked back around, and the two men fired together.

EIGHTEEN

Natalie was waiting for him. She looked pale and a little shaky, but when he pushed aside the curtain separating her examining table in the emergency room from the rest of the patients, the smile she lifted up to him was luminous nonetheless.

It was over, finally over. The aftermath had taken hours—a man, after all, was dead. But matching the shoe prints from the lakeshore to Brad's would confirm what Ginny's testimony and Brad's own admissions had already told them—Brad had murdered Ethan Parrish and had been behind the scheme of harassment against Natalie that had spiraled into kidnapping. A separate inquiry would address Miller's actions as a police officer. His bullet had killed Brad and, justifiable or not, an internal investigation was required.

"Hey, how are you doing?" Miller asked, approaching the table where Natalie sat, her legs swung over the side.

"I'm fine," she said softly.

Miller reached the examining table, moved his

hand to delicately touch the painful-looking lump at her temple where Brad had struck her with the gun. "Thank God," he said. "Thank God you really *are* fine now."

He put his arms around her, held her gently, just soaking in the miracle of having her with him. The horror of nearly losing her was still fresh. Someday the memories would fade, but he didn't believe he'd ever stop feeling this intensity of emotion when he was with Natalie.

His feelings hadn't diminished in ten years. He knew they would last forever, growing stronger all the time.

"Have you heard anything about Ginny?" she asked when he pulled back.

He nodded, keeping his arms around her, needing to keep up the contact between them. He wasn't ready to let go of her.

"She just came out of surgery. Luckily, Brad's bullet flew wide when he tried to turn back to grab you, and she was only hit in the shoulder. The statements she made at the site, before the ambulance loaded her up, are just the beginning for her, though. She has a lot of consequences to face, and she won't be going anywhere for a long time."

"I still can't believe it." Natalie shook her head. "Ginny tried to save me in the end. That means something to me, at least. But, Brad—"

She stopped, a painful emotion crossing her face. It would take time, Miller knew, for her to get over the betrayal she'd experienced. He wanted to be there, to help her through it.

"How are *you?*" she asked, changing the subject.

"Well, there'll be an administrative hearing, of course," he told her. "But that's routine. It just means I'll have some time off. I don't want you to worry about it." He expected to be cleared, but that wouldn't change his future. Only Natalie could do that.

"I'm going to worry about you, so forget it," she said determinedly. "You've worried enough about me. It's only fair that I get to worry about you a little bit now."

Miller smiled.

"Okay. You can worry—a *little* bit."

He leaned in to kiss her gently on the mouth, still apprehensive that she couldn't possibly be as fine as she said she was.

She'd nearly been killed. That would haunt him for a long time, he knew. And he would be thanking God every night that she hadn't been.

"Hold me tighter," she whispered. "I'm not going to break, I promise."

"I'm so glad you're all right," he whispered against her ear. "I can't imagine a single day without you. Not one. I love you."

She drew back slightly, lifted her gaze to him. "Oh, Miller." Reaching up, she touched his face, as if memorizing it bit by bit. "I love you, too." She took a deep breath. "But we have to talk."

He could see she was serious, and that she was upset. He took her hand. "I'm listening."

"Before this goes any further," she said quietly. "Before we start talking about the future, I want you to know that I might not be able to have kids." Her eyes were dark with an anguish he was only beginning to understand as she spoke. "It's possible I could get pregnant, but it's also possible that I won't. Ever. The doctors told me they weren't sure. All the treatments—" Emotion made her voice tremble, and she paused to steady it. "The treatments that saved my life might have made it impossible. We won't know till we try. I just want you to know that. I know how important family is to you, how much you want to have one of your own because of your childhood."

Miller's heart filled painfully. That she was worrying about him, when she was the one hurting, blew him away. He cupped her face tenderly.

"Natalie, sweetheart—" he started, but was stopped by a commotion beyond the curtain around Natalie's table.

Justus Buchanan's voice carried loud and clear across the emergency room. "I want to see my daughter now. I paid for half of this hospital, so don't think you're going to stand in my way."

The curtain swept aside and Natalie's father appeared, a harried-looking nurse hard on his heels. Miller stepped back.

Justus came forward, his gaze raking Natalie from head to toe. "Are you all right?" he demanded.

His voice was harsh, but Miller recognized the panic in Justus's voice. He was a big man, tall and fit, with a thick head of silver hair. As always, he presented a powerful presence, but for the first time, Miller detected something vulnerable on the older's man face—and he felt a kinship with him that surprised him. They both loved Natalie.

"I'm fine, Dad," Natalie said.

Miller could see her blinking back emotion, gathering strength.

"It's just a nasty bump, that's all," she went on. "They're releasing me as soon as they get the paperwork." The nurse hung back, looking fretful. "It's all right," Natalie said to her. The nurse cast Justus an irritated glance before disappearing with a flick of the curtain.

Justus's gaze transferred to Miller. "I understand I have you to thank for saving my daughter's life," he said.

"Your daughter didn't do such a shabby job of saving herself," Miller said. "I just showed up to help her finish the job."

"Well, I'm grateful." Justus extended his arm to Miller, shook hands briefly.

"I'll let you two talk," Miller said. He took Natalie's hand and squeezed it. "I'll be in the waiting room," he said firmly. "I'm not going anywhere without you. We're not finished talking." He kissed her cheek. "I love you."

The curtain swayed into place behind him, and she was alone with her father.

"What are you doing with that boy?" Justus stabbed the words at her.

She steeled herself for a blast of his dictatorial disapproval. "I think it's obvious he's not a boy," she said, lifting her chin. "He's a man. A good man."

"He's not good enough for you," he clipped out.

"He's *too* good for me," Natalie argued.

"No one is too good for you," Justus barked. "You're special. You're perfect. He'd be lucky to have you!"

Natalie blinked, taken aback. She was used to her father criticizing her. Praise was much more rare.

Justus's eyes glittered with what she realized with a shock were unshed tears.

"Maybe Miller *is* good enough for you," he said almost angrily, pacing in the confined space for a few seconds before turning abruptly and fixing his piercing glare on his daughter. He took a deep breath. "At least he has the courage to tell you how he feels. I was always too scared for that."

Natalie looked at him in surprise. "Scared?"

He stared up at the ceiling. "I was always afraid of losing you," he said in a subdued voice, his gaze coming back to her slowly. "I lost your mother, you see, and I could have lost you, too, that day." He looked pained. "You were in the car. I don't think I ever told you that. You were in the car when she died. It was a miracle you weren't hurt. She was killed, and you were all I had left."

He stared at her, seeming to take in her features one at a time. "I didn't know what to do with a little girl on my own. I loved your mother so much, and as you grew, you looked just like her. It hurt just to look at you sometimes."

Hot tears sprang to Natalie's eyes.

"It wasn't your fault," Justus went on roughly before she could say anything. "I was hurting, but that didn't make it right—the way I raised you. I was afraid of loving you too much. I was afraid of losing you. Your mother always drove too fast, and I never said a word to her about it. Always indulged her because of how I loved her. All I knew to do was surround you with rules and restrictions, anything to keep you safe."

Natalie moved without even realizing it, hopping down off the examining table to go to her father. She reached for his hands, so unused to touching him but needing to, just the same. All the barriers between herself and her father seemed to be exploding suddenly, leaving unexplored territory.

"I knew that you loved me," she said softly, emotion thick in her throat. "I just needed to hear it sometimes—that's all."

His arms wrapped around her. "I do love you, Natalie," he whispered. "When I found out what happened today—" He couldn't continue.

"I love you, too," she whispered.

Justus brushed at his eyes, and she realized he'd

been crying. She'd never seen him cry before, and she might never see him cry again. She knew that tomorrow he would be the same controlling, dictatorial man he was yesterday.

But the words they'd spoken today wouldn't go away. She would remember them forever.

"I want you to be happy," he said quietly. "Will he make you happy?"

She nodded, a lump filling her throat.

"Then go to him," Justus said. "He's waiting for you."

"Are you ready to go home?" Miller asked when she met him in the emergency waiting room.

Natalie's heart pinched.

"We need to talk," she said.

Miller pushed open one of the double glass doors that led out to the parking lot. Outside, dusk claimed the day in pink-gold clouds.

He took her hand and they began to cross the lot.

"We *are* talking," Miller said. "How would you feel about making the ranch your home?"

Natalie's breath caught sharply. She stopped dead in her tracks and stared at him.

"Aren't you going to say something?" He looked oddly, sweetly nervous.

"I don't know what to say."

"Say you'll marry me."

She felt giddy. "But—"

"There are no buts." He squeezed her hand. "The Farrells taught me what a real family is. It's about love, Nat. Not blood. If we can't have our own kids, we'll adopt. There are plenty of kids out there who need good homes. We'll fill the ranch house with kids, if that's what you want."

Tears rushed to her eyes. "I love you so much," she whispered.

"Then say you'll marry me," he said again, refusing to be sidetracked.

Joy ballooned in her heart. "Yes."

He smiled. "Then let's go home," he said, and he kissed her, right there, in the middle of the parking lot.

And she was home already.

BOOK YOUR PLACE ON OUR WEBSITE
AND MAKE THE
READING CONNECTION!

We've created a customized website just for our very special readers, where you can get the inside scoop on everything that's going on with Zebra, Pinnacle and Kensington books.

When you come online, you'll have the exciting opportunity to:

- View covers of upcoming books
- Read sample chapters
- Learn about our future publishing schedule (listed by publication month *and author*)
- Find out when your favorite authors will be visiting a city near you
- Search for and order backlist books from our online catalog
- Check out author bios and background information
- Send e-mail to your favorite authors
- Meet the Kensington staff online
- Join us in weekly chats with authors, readers and other guests
- Get writing guidelines
- AND MUCH MORE!

Visit our website at
http://www.zebrabooks.com

COMING IN JANUARY FROM
ZEBRA BOUQUET ROMANCES

#29 SAND CASTLES by Kate Holmes
__(0-8217-6457-8, **$3.99**) Artist Alys Vincent never expected to fall in love with the sun-bronzed hunk she'd approached on the beach to model for her. But when she found herself in Jerod's strong arms, she dared to dream that they could build a love more enduring than golden summer days . . . and sand castles.

#30 BENEATH A TEXAS MOON by Clara Wimberly
__(0-8217-6458-6, **$3.99**) Jessica McLean's girlhood crush on Diego Serrat had turned into grown-up passion—until he left her with a broken heart and a precious secret. Now, the tough Texas Ranger is back in town on assignment. His job—to protect her. But who will protect Jessica's heart?

#31 DANGEROUS MOVES by Mary Morgan
__(0-8217-6459-4, **$3.99**) Rodeo star Dillon McRay has lived his life on the principle that you only go around once. Now, he's determined to make the most of it—with beautiful Brooke Stephenson. Although she believes she's not the gambling type, Dillon's got to convince her that some chances are worth taking.

#32 A MATTER OF TRUST by Deb Stover
__(0-8217-6460-8, **$3.99**) Every man has a woman he can't forget, and for sexy veterinarian Gordon Lane, that woman is Taylor Bowen...back in Digby, Colorado, and more beautiful than ever. Can he and Taylor find the courage to reclaim an old love?

Call toll free **1-888-345-BOOK** to order by phone or use this coupon to order by mail.
Name _____
Address _____
City _____ State _____ Zip _____
Please send me the books I have checked above.
I am enclosing $_____
Plus postage and handling* $_____
Sales tax (in NY and TN) $_____
Total amount enclosed $_____
*Add $2.50 for the first book and $.50 for each additional book.
Send check or money order (no cash or CODs) to:
Kensington Publishing Corp., 850 Third Avenue, New York, NY 10022
Prices and Numbers subject to change without notice. Valid only in the U.S.
All books will be available 1/1/00. All orders subject to availability.
Visit our web site at **www.kensingtonbooks.com**

Put a Little Romance in Your Life With
Janelle Taylor

Celebrate Romance With Two of Today's Hottest Authors

Meagan McKinney

__In the Dark	$6.99US/$8.99CAN	0-8217-6341-5
__The Fortune Hunter	$6.50US/$8.00CAN	0-8217-6037-8
__Gentle from the Night	$5.99US/$7.50CAN	0-8217-5803-9
__A Man to Slay Dragons	$5.99US/$6.99CAN	0-8217-5345-2
__My Wicked Enchantress	$5.99US/$7.50CAN	0-8217-5661-3
__No Choice But Surrender	$5.99US/$7.50CAN	0-8217-5859-4

Meryl Sawyer

__Thunder Island	$6.99US/$8.99CAN	0-8217-6378-4
__Half Moon Bay	$6.50US/$8.00CAN	0-8217-6144-7
__The Hideaway	$5.99US/$7.50CAN	0-8217-5780-6
__Tempting Fate	$6.50US/$8.00CAN	0-8217-5858-6
__Unforgettable	$6.50US/$8.00CAN	0-8217-5564-1

Call toll free **1-888-345-BOOK** to order by phone, use this coupon to order by mail, or order online at **www.kensingtonbooks.com**.

Name _____

Address _____

City _____ State _____ Zip _____

Please send me the books I have checked above.

I am enclosing	$_____
Plus postage and handling*	$_____
Sales tax (in New York and Tennessee only)	$_____
Total amount enclosed	$_____

*Add $2.50 for the first book and $.50 for each additional book.

Send check or money order (no cash or CODs) to:

Kensington Publishing Corp., Dept. C.O., 850 Third Avenue, New York, NY 10022

Prices and numbers subject to change without notice.

All orders subject to availability.

Visit our website at **www.kensingtonbooks.com**.